THE PANDA HUNT

by the same author

A DANCE FOR THE MOON
KHALINDAINE

THE PANDA HUNT

Richard Burns

JONATHAN CAPE
THIRTY-TWO BEDFORD SQUARE
LONDON

First published 1987
Copyright © 1987 by Richard Burns
Jonathan Cape Ltd, 32 Bedford Square, London WC1B 3EL

British Library Cataloguing in Publication Data
Burns, Richard, 1958-
The panda hunt.
I. Title
823'.914[F]   PR6052.U66/

ISBN 0-224-02445-0

Phototypeset by Falcon Graphic Art Ltd
Wallington, Surrey
Printed in Great Britain by Biddles Ltd
Guildford and King's Lynn

for Karen

Contents

OLD WORLD

1

Monaco

It is Friday 2 August. My wife has been dead five months. I have nothing to do but write.

Dusk slumps over my exile. The room darkens. I switch on my desk lamp and the angle-poise poses, preying like a heron above its pool of light. My story begins. It begins here, in Monaco. This is as good a place as any to begin, I guess.

It was almost forty years ago; it was late 1926. I was in Europe to study at the Sorbonne, and taking my vacation with some people I knew from Cornell. We stayed at Cal's villa, a few miles along the coast from Monte Carlo. Christmas had happened and we waited for New Year; we were slung between the festivals like fairy lights, and were just as brightly lit. One night we went to the Casino. 1926 was the year Valentino died, Tunney beat Dempsey, Byrd flew over the Arctic and Baird demonstrated his 'television' in London. But, more clearly than any of these, I remember a room garnished with diamonds and a croupier spinning a wheel.

'Five,' I willed. 'Five, five.' It was my first time at the tables and I did not know then if it were better to stare at my stake or the wheel. Behind me were Clara and Tam, sharing my bet, my tension, and – they hoped – my beginner's luck.

The wheel rattled to silence; the ball was trapped and still.

'Cinq.'

The croupier scooped across the table. Some piles of

chips were devastated, but mine looked like Manhattan. Clara grinned: my beginner's luck had paid off and her faith in faith was vindicated. She separated her share of the winnings and sent Tam to order champagne. While she rearranged the turrets of chips between favoured numbers and the *noir* the croupier turned my way. I shook my head; my bet stayed where it was.

I could not expect to win again so when the wheel spun I looked away. I saw the gilded baroque ceiling and the oxymoronic weight of the chandeliers. The clatter became a hush and the croupier called 'Vingt-deux.'

Clara was exasperated; Tam, on his return, more patient. 'Spread your investments,' he advised, though I could not see the point of sober advice in a game of chance. Clara had lost as well. I guess I did not understand then how gamblers use these maxims to justify each loss, nor how trite sayings could be landmarks in a random territory. There is the Martingale system, for instance, whereby the punter, 'to recoup the loss', doubles the stake if he loses, or the d'Alembert, by which the stake is raised one after a defeat and lowered one after a win. No wonder Louis Blanc, who had founded the Monte Carlo Casino, claimed money paid out at the tables was only lent.

'Go through to the bar,' Tam suggested. 'Open the champagne. You'll feel better.'

The bar was panelled dark wood, and was too big. A man there watched me, but I am used to that: at the Casino doors, for instance, where they check the passports, I was kept waiting though Tam and Clara were passed straight through. The man who watched came over. I expected he would ask where I was from, as most do, but instead he asked if it had been a heavy loss. I had not known it showed.

'My first,' I replied.

He looked puzzled, then understood. 'His first,' he said addressing my bottle of fatuous champagne. His worn-out

British accent found consonants a problem. 'But what became of the old beginner's luck?'

'I won,' I said, 'before I lost.'

He nodded. His attention skidded like a gramophone needle. 'You always will,' he said.

We went back from the Casino in Cal's limousine. It had rained a little that night, and the Corniche glistened in our headlamps. As Cal shook a cocktail Tam talked about Red Grange. Grange had been the sporting sensation of the previous year. 'D'you know how much that man earnt in a single game last year?' Tam asked. '$30,000!' He was as proud as if he had made the money himself. '$30,000! And they say that when he met the President old Coolidge just complained he hadn't been able to get tickets for the big game.' Tam whistled to himself. 'What's that man going to do next year?'

We did not know either so we said nothing, and the car took us out of Monaco along the coast road. Suddenly we slewed at a bend. Like Cal, I sat with my back to the way we were heading, except when we skidded. 'Chrissakes!' called Cal. He squirmed in his dickey seat and tapped the glass that separated us from the driver. 'Bob! Can't you drive this goddam thing or what, Bob?'

Cal turned back to us. 'There!' he announced with satisfaction.

It was a very comfortable car. Between the rear facing seats the coach builders had set a cabinet into the walnut. Cal passed his shaker to Tilly, his wife that year, and drew from the cabinet five glasses. He handed them round: they were cool and aloof to the touch. 'Nice and steady now,' he called Bob through the window, and Bob toot-tooted his horn in acknowledgement. We cradled the glasses gingerly as Cal poured us a highball each. 'Arrow Pictures have given old Red a contract worth $300,000,' Tam was saying as Cal filled his glass. 'Imagine that.' Imagine. There was a lurch, a squeal, a jerk. The car

13

bounced and squeaked down a short slope. It stopped. A single wheel spun in the silence; it spun like a cliché, like roulette.

'Are you going to pour all that down my crotch?' demanded Tam.

Cal looked along the alien length of his own left arm. The shaker dripped contemptuously on Tam's tuxedo. 'Gee!' said Cal. 'What happened?'

'We left the road.' It has been remarked I have a gift for irony, when really it is only a liking for the truth. The two are often confused.

'Ask your driver what the hell he thinks he's doing,' said Tam.

Cal was glad to oblige. 'What the hell you think you're doing?' he asked, tapping the glass.

Bob climbed out the car and balanced on the fender. He looked round. 'We's got a flat,' he diagnosed.

Cal turned back to us. 'A flat,' he explained.

Tam wore a fur coat. It bristled. 'Haven't you got a spare?'

Cal was glad to turn away again. 'Haven't you got a spare?'

'Sure have, sir,' said Bob, climbing back in. 'But it ain't going to do no good. We's off the road and down the hill. Somebody's going to have to' push.'

'Push it yourself,' said Tam.

Lights signalled over the water. They did not shine for us. Cal mixed another cocktail. From time to time cars passed on the road above us: their headlamps were twin cones of illuminated rain. Then there were no more cars, and we went to sleep.

A motor-horn woke me. A pale unhealthy daylight peered through the windshield, the kind of daylight that has slept the night in an automobile. The horn sounded again.

Cal was blinking opposite me. 'Hello?' he said. He

14

shook his head and pushed down the glass next to him. 'Hel-lo-o!'

'Are you all right!' called a voice from above. I pushed my window down too, and saw a man in a light suit hailing us through a megaphone. Maybe the megaphone was in case we were deaf, or dead; we were only thirty feet away.

'You American?' asked Cal.

Bob spoke up. 'Tyre's bust, sir. We need a tow.'

'Hold it a moment there,' said the stranger. 'I've a rope in my trunk.' He stepped back from the edge and we heard his motor fire. He worked the shift and brought his automobile round: we saw him tie a rope to his fender. Our confidence in him was growing. His Rolls-Royce was bigger than ours.

He tossed the loose end of rope towards us, and used it to lower himself down. 'I guess you'll have to get out,' he warned, as he and Bob fastened up our automobile.

The ground was wet. So was the air. The fine rain soaked into our tuxedos. Bob started the engine and we leant our cautious weight against the front of the car. Bob gave it more gas, and jets of mud shot from beneath the wheels and lashed us. Then the cars began to move.

As the car sped up, Tam seemed to slow down. He lost a shoe in the mud, rocked on one leg, opened his mouth and eyes wide, and toppled into the furrows the car had left. We must have been feeling miserable because we barely laughed at all.

We followed the car to the road. 'Thanks,' Cal said to the stranger. 'I'm Cal Lomas, by the way, and this is my wife Tilly.'

'Pleased to meet you. I'm Roscoe Hamilton.'

'Roscoe Hamilton the big-game hunter?' asked Clara, and as she simpered I remembered where I had seen the name: in the photogravure sections of the tabloids, captioning pictures of a man in short pants with his foot on the neck of a lion. 'I do hope,' continued Clara, with the wit that had made her such a success at Vassar

College, 'that you won't be hunting us.'

'No,' said Roscoe Hamilton. 'I only hunt big game.' I was beginning to like him.

Tam cleared his throat and introduced himself. 'Tam Marshall,' he said, 'and my wife Clara.' They shook hands and turned to me. 'Edmund Sin.'

'Pleased to meet you,' I said.

'You're Chinese!'

Actually I am from Illinois. I smiled.

He smiled back. 'You remind me of Chicago,' is what I thought he said, and which I thought very perceptive, Chicago being my home town. What he probably said though, I realised later, was, 'You remind me of Chingachgook': Chingachgook, the Last of the Mohicans, is actually pronounced Chicago by those in the know. He continued. 'I'm going to China next year, hunting a special kind of black and white bear. Why don't you come along?' He sounded almost serious; he had sounded that way when speaking to Clara too. 'I'm told it's the last big game.'

He was coiling the rope between his fist and his elbow. 'You ought to be on your way,' he advised us. 'You could get a chill dressed that way this morning.' He replaced the coil in his trunk. 'I'll be seeing you,' he called, firing his engine. He climbed in. 'Bye now.' The car pulled smoothly away, accelerated along the straight and rounded a bend. We heard it long after we had stopped seeing it.

Tam whistled. 'So that was Roscoe Hamilton.'

We got back in Cal's car. The leather was cold through our wet pants, and felt tacky. Tam's dress pants, a mixture of Martini and mud, gave off a seaboard reek. 'Wasn't Hamilton one of the Ohio gang?' asked Cal. 'Mixed up with President Harding.'

'You're thinking of Calvin Hamilton, Roscoe Hamilton's father,' said Tilly.

'Was he one of the Westhouse Gun Hamiltons?' I asked.

'Sure,' said Cal. He quoted their famous slogan: 'The West was won with a Westhouse Gun.'

'You should have taken him up on his offer, Edmund,' said Tilly.

'To go to China with him, you mean? I don't suppose he meant it. I don't know anything about China.'

'Then maybe it's time you learnt,' she said. She laughed.

So did I.

It was a short journey back to Cal's villa. 'We could have walked,' said Cal.

'Oh yeah?' said Tam.

'Yeah.'

'You never finished about Red Grange,' said Tilly.

We walked from the car. Cal carried his cocktail shaker; Tam talked about Red Grange. I did not listen to what he had to say; I was too busy thinking about China. But I did not miss anything. The next year belonged to Babe Ruth, and everyone forgot Red Grange.

I had not given my ancestry too much thought till then, I guess. Being Chinese was kind of an aberration, like buck teeth or crabapple cheeks; everyone I met was white, except servants who were mostly black. Sure, I saw other Chinese occasionally, in laundries or as the bad guys in movies, but I had never met another Chinese boy from my background. And I had never, ever, met a Chinese girl.

There were times, looking in the mirror, I almost surprised myself. The costume was familiar enough: those were the days of the Brooks Brothers suit, worn with starched collars and pastel ties; all around me were such suits, such shirts, such ties. It was the face that was different. It was rounded and hairless: it was almost, in the presence of all those angular European features, more like the outside mould for a face than a face itself. And though I was popular, no girls ever fell for that fat harvest moon; and had they done, there was a network of matrons coast-to-coast ready to cry 'What about the children!' at the first kiss. My contemporaries had petting parties and convertibles; I had uninvited confidences and the privacy of the washroom. In short, I was, at twenty-three, a college-educated, popular, intelligent, castrated leper.

In China, I realised, I would be cured and healed.

We drank bourbon on New Year's Eve. I used to read H. L. Mencken's radical *American Mercury* magazine in those days, and knew the world could be a better place. 'To 1927!' I offered.

Tam was committed heavily on Wall Street. '1927!' he replied.

'President Coolidge!' toasted Cal.

'Prosperity!' said Tilly.

'The States!' said Tam.

'Hollywood!' said Cal. The bourbon smelt sweet, childhood candy and liquor licorice, but its taste was warm and experienced. We smiled at one another. 'I want to swim,' Cal declared.

'Sure,' said his wife.

'I do! Come on! Let's go down the plage!'

We changed into our bathing costumes in the villa and followed the path to the beach. The path was sandy, the beach stony, and the pebbles were dank underfoot. In the end only Clara went swimming, while the rest of us paddled in the shallows and let the old year drain out between our toes.

Clara came out of the sea, shaking water from her bobbed hair and trying to smooth her goose-bumps flat. 'I want to go to the Casino,' she said.

'Oh yeah,' said her husband. 'Sleep in the car again, huh?'

'Be quiet, Tam. I want to go to the Casino. Who's coming?'

We were almost out of whisky. There was only red wine left. It was time that we moved on.

We accelerated along the coast road. 'There'll be all sorts of people there tonight,' said Tilly. 'I guess Douglas Fairbanks'
            'and Mary Pickford'
                        'and Somerset Maugham'
'and Lady Cunard'
            'and Charlie Chaplin'
                        'and Michael Arlen'
        'and Gerald Murphy'
                    'and Mrs Murphy'
                            'and Gloria Swanson'
            'and Coco Chanel'
                        'and the Duke of Westminster'
                    'who everyone calls Bendor'
                            'and Scott Fitzgerald'
            'and Mrs Laura Corrigan – '
                        'Who?'
                            'Mrs Laura Corrigan'
            'the social climber'
                        'who was a telephone girl'
'from Cleveland, Ohio'
            'and married well.'
    'Oh. That Laura Corrigan.'

We were passing a long white painted wall that gathered what little light was left in the night and conserved it. 'Isn't that Roscoe Hamilton's place?' said Cal.

'Stop!'

They looked at me. 'You going to be sick?' asked Clara.

'I'm going to see Hamilton. He's going to take me to China.'

'It's too far,' said Tam, 'to get tonight.'

The car stopped. 'Take a couple of bottles,' said Cal.

'You're a friend,' I told him as he handed me the wine. I stood on the running board, clasped a bottle beneath each arm, and leapt. 'Have a Happy New Year!'

'And you!'

I watched them drive away.

There was a dusty margin of grass between the wall and the road, and no sign of a gate. 'Which way?' I asked myself. A car came up the highway from Monaco, its headlamps glaring at me, flaring at me, and then it passed, only to stop suddenly a few hundred feet away and reverse back.

'Ed!' said Cal's voice.

'You've come back,' I said.

'Forgot to give you this.'

Something landed at my feet; as the car turned in the road its lamps identified a corkscrew in the gutter. I picked it up, thoughtfully. I looked at the wall and decided I could climb it. Putting the bottles in my pocket I reached up, grasped, climbed and toppled. I was over: I was lucky. All I broke was a bottle.

I made my way through cypresses until I reached a hardtop drive. Up the hill above me I could make out a villa. There were no lights showing.

I reached the out-buildings. What had once been a stable was now a garage. I looked through a window in the wooden doors and saw spiders' webs. I carried on up towards the house.

It was a humourless, classical villa. Between two pillars was a large white-painted door, and to the side of the door was a bell-pull. I pulled. A long way off I heard a ring.

A light came on in a basement room. I waited a spell and heard bolts being drawn. The door opened a crack.

'Hi,' I said. 'Is Mr Hamilton home?'

The door closed and re-opened; a safety-chain, I realised. 'M. Hamilton is away,' said a voice in French. 'The house is closed.'

I was speaking to a thin handsome woman of fifty or so. 'Will he be back soon?' I asked.

'No.'

'Ah. Well, I guess I'd better be on my way.'

'You are Chinese,' she decided. 'It is for the panda.' I was surprised to realise she approved of me. 'Come in. You have come a long way. You must see the trophies.'

'Thank you.'

She lit an oil lamp and led me through marble halls. The flame echoed off polished surfaces and planes. The furniture cowered beneath white sheets. We reached a pair of wide doors and stopped.

She had a bunch of keys fastened tight to her belt. With a sensuous twitch she pressed one to the lock and opened the doors.

'Oh!'

The lamplight stretched out to a lion, crouching before it leapt. Its eyes were fixed at my throat.

'Oh,' I repeated, on a lower note. 'It's stuffed.'

'Mounted,' she corrected. She went up to the lion and stroked her fingers through its mane. The hair looked artificial; the lamplight made it cheap. 'A maneater,' she continued. 'It took seventy-three victims before M. Hamilton caught up with it.'

There was a candelabrum on the mantelshelf. She lit a candle with a match, and used that candle to light the others. The walls of the room were studded with animal heads.

'Seventy-three?' I said. I felt the benign glass eyes of the animals watching me. When she had said trophies I had thought of silver cups.

'Railway employees for the most part. But one or two white men.'

· 'It's beautifully stuffed – mounted.'

'The work of a man in Dresden. Dead now. He killed himself. And they found the bodies of seven women in the cupboards of his house.' She paused. 'All mounted.' I still do not know if she was joking. 'Now you must look round,' she instructed.

By each head was a label which gave a Latin classification, a location and a date. Bengal, Brazil, Borneo; Kenya, Kentucky, Kabul. Several of the places meant nothing to me; others were quite familiar. I was surprised at the label by one grizzly head: 'Mount Corkery, Col., May 12, 1898'.

'Ah! You have noticed! Monsieur's first grizzly. He shot it when he was nine. His grandfather was terribly proud. He told the young man he would grow up to be the greatest hunter in the world, and he was right.'

'Mmmmm,' I agreed.

She led me away and pointed out various exhibits. She showed me one among a group of tigers' heads. 'Another maneater – this was said to have taken more than sixteen hundred natives in five years. M. Hamilton was two months stalking it.'

'Mmmmmmm.' I tried to look enthusiastic but I could not like that room. The glass eyes were too forgiving and incurious for me: they stared across their plush mausoleum with neither venom nor wit, and said nothing of life or death or what it must be to be a tiger. I turned for relief to the group of photographs arranged around the hearth. At least the animals here looked as if they had once been alive, if only because now they looked so dead. I saw Roscoe Hamilton astride a huge tiger's corpse, surrounded by flies; with a friend in huge shorts above a dead rhino; by the body of an elephant whose entrails spilt in fat moist heaps like piles of discarded condoms. Like the trophies, the photographs were all labelled:

22

'Rahjapura, Bengal, February 17, 1914'; 'Qalla, New Guinea, July 9, 1922'; 'Old Hickory, Oregon, June 18, 1908'. One, 'The Day's Bag, Mongalowri', described a long thin photograph, the kind found in yearbooks, of hundreds of dead bison lying in rows and being picked over by natives in short pants.

The only variation I could find was a photograph of Warren Harding, the previous president. I recalled what Tam had said about Harding being a friend of Hamilton's father, and smiled when I read the caption. 'Warren Harding. Pres. United States of America, d. August 2, 1923.' Harding, it seemed, had joined the trophies.

– A coincidence. Today is also August 2, and Harding has been dead forty years –

I left soon after, through the ghosts of covered Louis XIV furniture and the gleaming of marble walls. My bourbon bravado had worn off and I wondered how I was going to get home. I reached the road and turned back towards Cal's. The area was rich with handsome villas, the millionaire homes of the millionheirs. The sky had cleared, and the moon made faces on the sea.

It was cold. I still had a bottle of wine in my pocket, I discovered: I shall drink a little, I decided, while I wait for Cal and the rest of the guys to drive back from Monaco.

Instead I drank it all, and awoke the following morning. It was a bright morning and the sun was already clear of the mountains. I could see Cal's villa, nipple-pink on a distant headland. It was not a long walk.

The others were still asleep. I decided to go to bed.

Pretty soon after my vacation was finished. I said goodbye to Tilly and Cal, Clara and Tam, and returned to Paris on the Train Bleu. The others were going back to the States. The Riviera season was ended, and though Scott Fitzgerald and the Murphies had already scandalised the natives by staying on the beaches through the summer, my Cornell buddies were not of such pioneering stuff.

Theirs was second generation wealth. They were on their way back home.

I travelled to Paris overnight, and woke to racing fields and pastel towns. Sometimes we went through stations; sometimes we crossed quiet rivers. I climbed from my bunk and cleaned my teeth in the folding basin. Outside, the shuttered houses were like sleeping children. I was finishing my first cigarette when the train pulled into Paris.

I shall keep Paris for another day though. It is past midnight now in Monaco, and across the wad of paper that lies, bloated and blanched in my angle-poised pool, I have written too much already. My back hurts and so does my head. I hear voices in the street, calling one another, but no one calls for me. At twenty-three I learnt to dream of China. Now I am fifty-nine, and would prefer a dreamless sleep.

2
Paris

I roomed in the Sixth *arrondissement*. I went from the station by cab and when I got there I saw a war veteran playing his violin in the street and plaited water running in the gutter.

The veteran played the old songs. 'Aïe, aïe, aïe, j'ai mal aux dents.' Round his neck was a sign saying he had lost his sight at Verdun, but when I gave him a coin he said, 'Merci, monsieur le chinois.'

The apartment block smelt of tobacco and lavender. I climbed the stairs, passing the bicycles tethered on each landing. My rooms were at the top of the flight. I let myself in. The concierge, Mme Villois, had started a fire for me. I was glad. I sat in front of it and shook off my shoes and the room was the colour of dried flowers. It was raining outside: the window was guarded by drapes that bulged above their tassels and rationed the cheap city light. It was becoming dark already; twilight: *le crépuscule*. The clock ticked. Second Empire furniture straddled African rugs. I had taken the room furnished; this taste was not mine. In the grate the Belgian coal smoked, glowered and sagged. I lit a cigarette and tossed the match into the flames.

I had developed a routine the previous semester. I left my rooms at eight-thirty and went downstairs to check my mail; Mme Villois looked at me, scowled and, I swear, crossed herself. I cannot say I enjoyed this curious ritual.

My street led into the rue de Fleurus, where Gertrude Stein and her lover lived. Gertrude Stein was well-known

25

for her hospitality to young Americans abroad in France; passing her studios I always whistled Gershwin. She lived at number twenty-seven. I was never invited in.

At the end of the rue de Fleurus is the Palais du Luxembourg where, in those days, the Cézannes were hung. I rarely looked at them; I did like the gardens though. The paths were gravel and shifted and shrugged underfoot. The trees were bare at that time of year but the air was clear.

The walk through the Luxembourg gardens took me almost directly to the university, but I generally walked straight by, down the boulevard St-Michel to the Seine. There was a café I knew on the quai de Montebello, opposite the Île de la Cité, and I had breakfast there. Everyone who has lived in Paris recommends a little café they know that is off the beaten track, that is quintessentially French yet subtly superior; it is a matter of honour to find one for oneself. Mine was at an intersection facing the cathedral. The proprietor had picked up some American slang from U.S. Servicemen in the war; I was his first American customer since *les doughboys* had left, and I got his personal attention, his best table, and overcharged. Through the blank spaces where the window artists had lettered a huge blue tobacco advertisement I could see the crouching back of Notre Dame. It was made of a more intricate stone than the rest of Paris, and patterned itself with shadows.

After my *café complet* I went to the university. I was studying Voltaire. I share a birthday with Voltaire, but I have never known if this is important. Had I told my tutor that I sometimes wondered if I studied Voltaire because of the coincidence of our birthdays he would have been scornful. M. Péloueyre prided himself on his rationality. He had a good mind that was always working, always making connections: he saw congruence where I saw chaos. For instance, according to my guidebook the Luxembourg palace had been built for Marie de' Medici in the style of her native Florence but, as I remarked to M. Péloueyre, to me it looked typically French.

'This is because you do not know which details are significant, nor which differences matter.' We spoke, as we often did, in English. 'The way we come to terms with the world is by differentiation; we learn to distinguish the things that matter to us. If one is to understand understanding, it is necessary to comprehend the notion of *significant difference*.' He looked up from his desk at me, almost slyly. 'You accept, I suppose, that what we call "reality" is not an absolute but is a construct dependent on the information provided by our imperfect senses? Think how a dog must perceive reality: a hound's nose is fabulously powerful and can detect nuances of smell where we can detect nothing at all. The model of reality constructed by a dog, in other words, is defined by odours we cannot even perceive.'

There is a kind of intellect which sees man born free but spoilt by circumstance; there is a different cast of mind which sees him as a monster held in check by the rigour of society. For both, society is oppressive but, for the second type, necessarily so. M. Péloueyre's mind was of the second type. There were many in France after the First World War who would have agreed.

'Secondly,' he continued, 'you must accept that the ability to differentiate is a vital one to the success of the species. This is axiomatic. The moth which cannot tell a candle flame from a potential mate will never rule the world; the emperor who knows which of his advisers is lying might.

'Thirdly, whilst it has been biologically determined that a dog's nose will be different to ours, I doubt there is anything biological about your failure to distinguish between the architecture of the Palais de Luxembourg and that of the rest of Paris. Culture, not nature, is responsible here.

'Myself, I was born in the Gironde, near Bordeaux. My

27

father was the schoolmaster at La Brède, where Montesquieu lived: while I studied Montesquieu's letters under my father's tutelage my schoolmates learnt about the soils of the region and the varieties of grape; while I learnt the vocabulary of eighteenth-century discourse they learnt the argot of the wine-grower; while I learnt to identify the characteristic modes of thought in the seventeenth and eighteenth centuries they were learning to distinguish vintages and vineyards.

'Or, to give you another example, think of accents. A Parisian can doubtless tell someone from the place de la Contrescarpe from someone from the slums behind St Lazare. I cannot do that, though I can at least identify the accents of each of the major cities of France. You, as an American, probably cannot do even that: although your French is good you cannot, I imagine, tell between accents except on broad lines of north and south, educated and uneducated. To take this further, someone with no French may well be able to recognise the language when they hear it, just as I think I can recognise Russian; and someone who cannot do that may not even be certain it is a language they hear at all, just as I can make no sense of the jumbled noise of Punjabi or Hindi.

'Yet those differences must be there for each of us to perceive. Our ears are anatomically much the same. We hear the same things, but attach different significances to what we each hear. Likewise the eyes. We all see the colour of a woman's hair, but whereas for me, growing old and unconcerned about such matters, hair colour is not important, there are many men who are attracted only to blondes. For me it is more important that I should be able to tell an authentic manuscript from a fake or, should I need to borrow money, a Christian from a Jew. In short,' M. Péloueyre finished, 'the distinctions we make are vital to us; and, to take this one step further, the distinctions we make also define us, for all our outward perceptions and all the things that establish us in the world are the products of our ability to find significant differences.'

I remember that day as particularly cold. I walked back to my room. As I walked I thought. I thought about how I was significantly different in most people's eyes, although I talked like an American, dressed like an American, had been educated like an American. I thought too about how my father seemed to be unaware of the difference between me and white Americans. He recognised that *he* was different, but put that down to the fact that he had been born in the Orient. I was a native of Chicago. I was his all-American boy.

I left the gravel path and, lighting a cigarette, wandered into the scrawny shade of the trees. The grass had failed completely there and, though it was early in the year, the earth was cracking. M. Péloueyre had talked of hair colour, and I realised it was true that amongst Europeans the colour of a man's hair mattered no more than the colour of his tie. But surely at some stage in Europe's past, when there were Jutes and Vandals and Romans and Celts all fighting, this distinction would have been vital?

I dropped my cigarette and hurried back to my apartment. I was excited. For the first time in my life I had a way of judging other people's reaction to me that did not leave me feeling the oddball.

I had been invited out that evening by the Drummonds of Baltimore. Mrs Drummond helped the same charities as my mother. I changed and telephoned for a cab.

The Drummonds lived north of the river. I had never met them; Mrs Drummond, I guess, wanted a fourth for bridge. I had imagined life in Paris to be full of parties where artists' models sang the blues and bearded poets discussed James Joyce: instead it was nights in with my books or weak exiled cocktails in cosy drawing rooms. I reached the place, paid off my cab and rang the bell.

I could hear loud jazz and voices. I envied the partygoers; I wondered if they could do with a fourth for bridge. I rang the bell again. Perhaps no one had heard.

Almost at once the door opened. 'Hello,' said a smiling man. His bow tie was unfastened and its loose ends were fish tails. 'Glad you could make it.' He swayed towards me and away, swelling in my vision as if I were the drunk. 'Come right in.'

He led me up the stairs. A gramophone spun out stylised, sterilised white jazz. We passed a girl in a red dress. We had to climb over her legs. When my companion opened the door ahead I saw dancers wrapped in elegant swirls of tobacco smoke and heard the saxophone playing low. A girl with a cigarette in her long holder smiled at me and her tongue traced slowly round her lips.

'You want a drink?' I was led to a table loaded with bottles. The bottles were mostly empty.

'Is this the Drummond apartment?' I asked.

'Eh?'

'Drummond. Of Baltimore.'

'Hey Jack. Guy here wants to know if this is the Drummond apartment.'

'Of Baltimore,' I added.

'Say,' replied Jack. 'Aren't they the people lived upstairs? The ones went away because of the noise?'

'Sure. That's them. Knew I knew the name.'

'Nasty, militaryish sort of name, Drummond,' mused an Englishman with a Ronald Coleman moustache.

'We're almost out of drink,' announced the man who had opened the door on me, and he and Jack left, arguing about what should be done about the situation.

'Is that true?' asked the Englishman.

'There's some whisky left in this bottle,' I suggested.

'Thank you. I say, you should have seen this place when the party started. Crates of the stuff. Marvellous. You wouldn't happen to have a cigarette on you, by the way? Oh, thanks awfully. Such a bore to run out.'

I lit his cigarette and one for myself. 'What time did the

30

party start?' I asked, looking at the débris.

'Wednesday.'

I offered him the bottle. 'Hardly enough in there for a couple of chaps like us,' he said. 'What say you we clear off before the rest of the inebriates discover the absence of drink.'

He took me to a place where we ordered champagne. 'Six glasses,' he instructed. He lined them up along the table and filled them all. 'Last one to down three buys the next bottle.' We drank four bottles that way, and I paid for them all.

I no longer knew where I was. I no longer cared. We had moved on several times. 'Splendid, splendid,' said my companion, and white-skinned willing women undressed before our eyes.

I ran a hand over my face, which did nothing to help. There was a girl on the Englishman's knee, but I do not know where we met her. Never mind. Concentrate on the stage. I nodded sagely to myself. The stage was worth concentrating on. But then the curtains were closed and I was weaned from the breasts.

'I say, old chap,' said the Englishman.

A drum began to roll. The curtains opened again. A lovely woman with long blonde hair was tied defenceless to a stake. It said 'Jeanne d'Arc' in sequins on the backdrop, and friendly warm lights played at being flames.

'I say, I hope you won't think this impertinent.'

The stage began to revolve slowly. Beneath the blonde hair she was naked.

'I say, I hope you won't think this impertinent, but you are Chinese aren't you?'

I licked my lips. 'Yes.' The stage revolved, allowing us to inspect St Joan.

'Thank God for that. I thought my eyes were playing up again.'

31

The front of my dress pants pumped with a kind of pain. I watched the woman burn, and then the ties that bound her fell free. She stepped forward and flung her hair back.

I had never seen a completely naked woman before. She was white flesh and shadows that intrigued, breasts, belly, buttocks, and the places I could not name. She moved, gyrated, pulsated, and then I became aware of the slippery stickiness in my undershorts.

'Another bottle, old man?' asked the Englishman, but I was devastatingly sober now.

'I'm going home.'

'What's the matter? Not feeling ill? Oh dear, oh dear! I see! You've ejaculated.' I had not known the word. 'Best come with me, old chap. That's the way.'

We walked out, he with an elegant drunken swagger and I with a napkin clasped to my groin. The girl hung from his shoulder like a pelisse. She was grinning.

'Where do you live?' asked the Englishman as he hailed a cab.

I told him and he told the driver. 'Accidents happen, old boy,' he said as he helped me in. 'Don't think any more of it. But, I say, you couldn't leave a chap a bob or two before you go? Nothing excessive: cab fare home, that sort of thing?' I handed him my wallet without speaking. I did not dare to speak. He counted out some notes and returned it, leaving me what I would need to pay for my journey. 'Au revoir,' he said, but I never saw him again. I never even learnt his name.

That night I died and, though the rigor mortis was loosening its grip, by the time I awoke I was well decomposed.

I climbed out of bed. I shall feel better soon, I decided, but felt worse. My bowels lurched. I went over to the shutters and opened them, but daylight kills the living dead and it was killing me. I lay back down on the bed.

Squashed up inside me, between my liver and colon, I felt guilt and shame, but like all the other messages I was receiving from my guts, this one was confused. I sat up and reached for a cigarette, and then remembered what had happened. I lit the cigarette and I felt terrible.

By Monday I could face the world, almost. I went in to the university and found my seminar was cancelled: the pope had denounced a right-wing organisation M. Péloueyre supported, and my professor was in shock or mourning. I did not care. The cancellation meant I would not have to think, and not thinking suited me fine.

It became a packed, dark, hurried semester. I vowed never to visit a nightclub again. My resolution lasted a week. After that I became an habitué of several, though my favourite was the Folies Bergère. It was expensive, but the girls were more attractive. I still have a programme from those days. M. Derval was in charge. M. Derval liked his dancers to be individuals. In America a chorus line is chosen for its uniformity, and looks like a fantasy concocted by Henry Ford; M. Derval's girls were unique, and when they smiled we loved them.

At the back of the Folies was a promenade, where the hookers strutted. It took me three visits to pluck up the courage. She was a pleasant lady of great experience. I was glad that I was normal, and sad I had to pay.

I found myself thinking of China again, in a wistful, foolish way. I had lost interest in my work. Fortunately, so had my professor. He was still fretting over Pope Pius XI and *Action française*.

It was party time the world over, and while America whooped it up on illicit hooch the European parties were quieter and more exclusive: the Nazi party, for instance, or *Action française* in France. The world was a fragile place and there was something desperate about the fun.

Charles Maurras, the right-wing intellectual, was the leader of *Action française*. He was anti-republican and anti-semitic; M. Péloueyre wanted him to become France's Mussolini.

'I have made a discovery,' he told me one day near Easter. 'I have found the source of Europe's ills.' I did not admire M. Péloueyre's politics but I did admire his intellect. In the almost innocent days before the Holocaust we thought it possible to separate the two. I listened carefully as he continued. 'I have discovered something that undermines all European history, M. Sin. I have discovered Christianity to be a Jewish plot.'

Mine is meant to be an inscrutable race. I think I probably gawped.

'It is true,' he went on. 'Christianity is a modified form of Judaism, made acceptable for Western minds. Notice the parallel here with Marxism. In both cases the initial idea is entirely Jewish, but as Marxism has spread throughout Europe in the diluted but still pernicious form of Socialism, so Judaism was disseminated in the form of Christianity. You see the marvellous logic?

'The role of the Catholic Church has been ambivalent in this. On the one hand its central precepts of love and forgiveness have been weakening Europe's natural strength for two thousand years, but on the other hand that natural strength has survived, for no amount of Jewish cunning could sap it entirely. Indeed, in the glorious era when the papacy was controlled by the Franks, who of all the peoples of Europe are the most noble and potent, the Jewish influence was curtailed and rendered virtually ineffectual. The Franks are naturally antipathetic to anything that stinks of Judaism. This was the age of chivalry and crusades; sadly, the Roman strain has lost its vitality, which is why Pius, so misguidedly, failed to endorse *Action française*. Even Mussolini, so admirable a man in many ways, does not I think fully comprehend the nature of the Jewish threat.

'You are a non-European Edmund, which is why I believe you, of all people, will recognise the truth of what

34

I say. Your mind has not been constrained by two thousand years of believing in a Jewish Messiah. It is a shame you wouldn't be allowed to our meetings; I'm sure you'd be interested. Unfortunately, however, our racial rules are necessarily very strict. But perhaps nevertheless you would like to read some of the literature of the cause. If you read German you'll find many whose research backs up my theories, although, sadly, no one but myself has yet recognised the threat posed by Christianity.' He smiled contentedly. 'We are not alone in our struggle,' he told me. 'All over Europe there are those willing to lay down their lives for the cause of freedom.'

Abandoned, I walked out of the university and turned towards the Seine, then followed the river east. Greasy, smoky cars drove by and the air tasted of dirt. I looked up out of the city. The sky was troubled and so was I: the clouds squeezed round the sun and burst it like an egg, spilling it in yolky veins.

I walked on, into the boulevards by the zoo. Old men tossed balls in the dust. They stank of captive animals. Everything did. I reached Austerlitz, crossed the *place*, and entered the station. A negro swept round my feet. When a European says Jew an American hears nigger. I thought of lynch-mobs and Klansmen, and of those I had heard in Chicago say that if the ghettoes of South Side and the Loop were razed then the town would be a cleaner place. I put my hand in my pocket and felt for change, but when I offered it to the negro he backed away frightened. There is a lot of prostitution at Austerlitz. Perhaps he thought I wanted a woman. Perhaps he was right, but I bought a newspaper instead.

I was tired of France. I picked out the London *Times*, which was the first paper in English I saw, and took it to a nearby café. I sat on the sidewalk drinking lukewarm coffee and reading yesterday's paper, the day before yesterday's news. Above me, the sky was still cheap food

35

and the clouds were the colour of lard. I read without expectation or interest. It was only when I saw a half-familiar name that I noted what I was reading at all: among the guests of Lord Hewcoate next week will be the renowned American sharpshooter and big-game hunter, Mr Roscoe Hamilton, or words to that effect. I thought of Roscoe Hamilton, and I thought of China.

I am, sometimes, a methodical man. I tore the article from the newspaper, counted out the price of the coffee and added a tip, and returned to the university. It took me some time to find what I was looking for in this unfamiliar section of the library. The giant panda, I discovered, looks like a black and white bear, though it is believed to be unrelated to the bears. Full grown, it is some four or five feet in length and it weighs over two hundred pounds. It is found only in the range of mountains that forms the western boundary of the great Red Basin of Szechuan, and is extremely rare.

I went back to my room. I decided I ought to write to my father, to tell him what was happening. Not that I knew myself. I picked up my pen and thought. I wanted to say, Dad, the concierge crosses herself each time she sees me and my professor thinks the Jews are a cancer; but I did not. My father was a proud man: he was proud of his all-American boy. Were I to admit I was not all-American, admit that despite the fortune he had spent on dressing me and educating me I was still entirely and absolutely Chinese in the eyes of most people, admit too that I had un-American sympathies for the underdog and suspected that all men were, despite evidence to the contrary, equal, I guess I would have broken his heart. So I wrote instead that I was going to London for the Easter vacation, and would write him again when I got there, and meantime would he give my love to my mother.

3
England

The setting sun projects a crimson patch the shape of the window against my wall and reminds me I must fasten my mosquito net. It is September now, and the mosquitoes are at their worst.

September: it took a single night to write my first chapter; my second has taken a month. I must work faster. November 24 is my sixtieth birthday. I want to have completed this by then; a man of sixty should be done with his youth.

It is time to meet Roscoe again. But first, some family history. His grandfather had founded the Hamilton fortune: John Hamilton emigrated from Scotland in 1863 and found a job with a Baltimore gunsmith called Alexander Westhouse. Westhouse was a talented man and Baltimore an opportune location: the Civil War raged round them with such confusion that Westhouse had clients in both armies, until fortune began to favour the Union, and then so did Westhouse. The business prospered, and so did Westhouse's protégé: by the time Lee surrendered at Appomattox Hamilton ran the business while his employer perfected a new gun; the Westhouse 'Modern' repeater was patented in 1869, the year Hamilton opened a new factory in Pittsburgh.

Though the Civil War was over there was still a market for a quick-firing, accurate and economical rifle; like all America at that time, Westhouse looked West. The Great Plains were being opened up, that immense grassland running from the Rockies to Longitude 98° East, from Texas to the Canadian border. It was a land of opportunity.

Hamilton was a good man where opportunity was concerned. He opened a network of dealerships both East and West of the Plains. The closing frontier could be plotted on a map of moving Westhouse franchises. He coined the famous slogan 'The West was won with a Westhouse gun', or at least claimed to have coined it. He sponsored rodeos in St Louis and Independence to advertise the rifle. He founded a magazine that celebrated the feats of cowboys toting Westhouse 'Moderns'.

After the Indians had been cleared, maimed and resettled it was necessary to divide up the spoils. The Westhouse Gun Company became the Westhouse Corporation. A factory in Philadelphia manufactured thousands of miles of barbed wire in the Westhouse name. The barbed wire stitched across the country. It sewed it up. By 1893 the Westhouse Corporation was the largest single property owner in five states, and ran everything from the railroads to the elections in three.

Somewhere along the way Hamilton bought his old boss out. He also married. His wife was of that kind which is too good for this world, and died producing the couple's only child.

Calvin Alexander Hamilton was handsome, profligate, charming and drunk. Behind every American drunk is an American dream, I guess, though rarely can this relationship have been clearer than in the case of young Calvin. Calvin married an 'actress' called Constance. She was the sort of actress that always gets inverted commas round the word, and some claimed, with equally heavy inverted commas, that she had once been a 'hostess'. They married in Paris, and when John Hamilton heard he promptly cut off his son's allowance. 'Married!' he said. 'She must be a bigger fool than Calvin!'

She was not quite the fool her father-in-law suspected, however. At the wedding she had been rather overweight for a woman in such an active profession: only Calvin was surprised when, five months later, young Roscoe appeared; he came home from a five-day bender, heard the baby wailing, and promptly made his five days ten. Constance already knew, however, where her son's future lay. She wrote to John Hamilton, saying what a fine boy Roscoe was becoming, and how like his grandfather. She detailed his teething and his needs. While her husband chased cold turkeys from under the bed, Constance offered John Hamilton the child, and even though her letters were unacknowledged, she persevered. While posing, wearing nothing but more inverted commas, for several 'artistic' photographs, she persuaded the photographer to take a snapshot of Roscoe, which she sent to John Hamilton. He still did not write to her, but he must have been moved: he sent his chauffeur all the way to Paris to collect the kid. Constance handed over her year old son and left this narrative for good. Which is a shame. She was an interesting, and possibly even a good, woman.

Roscoe was another sharp investment for John Hamilton. Initially withdrawn, the boy responded to expensive care and shot his first bear at nine. I had seen its head. Old John was delighted: inappropriately though sentimentally he nicknamed Roscoe 'Deerslayer', after the Fenimore Cooper character, and told the boy to go ahead and prove himself a Hawkeye; Roscoe responded by becoming to shooting what Popeye is to spinach.

Not that I knew the whole story when I quit Paris and took the boat-train to London. But then, neither did Roscoe.

London was dirtier than Paris. I took a cab between stations and we drove down the cracks between buildings. The walls of the buildings were grids that framed tall windows, but through the windows I saw only more walls.

There was a stall at the second station that sold maps. I

bought one, and discovered Norfolk was a county rather than a town; a place called Norwich sat in the middle of the county like a spider in a web. I went by railway, and it was dark when I arrived.

Norwich was a pleasant, flint-sided town. It smelt of breweries. I asked about Lord Hewcoate and was told I meant Lord Huckot and that, yes, he lived not far from the town. But I didn't mean Lord Huckot, I told them; they spelt Huckot for me and I found that I did. Cities are cities the world over, but Norwich was entirely England and I was a stranger there. I spent the night at a public house and drank a glass of warm beer with my supper. In the morning I hired a trap.

Lord Hewcoate's house was called Gulthorpe Hall. Gulthorpe was pronounced Gulthorpe. I rang the bell and a footman answered: Mr Hamilton was staying but was currently with his Lordship on the range; would I care to wait? I said I would go look for them.

I knew virtually nothing about shooting, and know very little still, but I did know a range must be a shooting range, and that where there is a shooting range there will be noise. I followed the noise. The reports clapped quickly and forgivably, coming and going and leaving little behind. I traced them to an ugly low building with asbestos walls. It looked like a shed; it sounded like the St Valentine's Day Massacre.

There was a window in the door and I peered in. Under the sharp light of naked electric bulbs five men in sleeveless sweaters were firing effortless pistols down the length of the shed. I knocked but no one heard. I walked in.

The noise was louder inside, but when I entered it stopped. I was grateful for the silence, but it embarrassed me.

'Mr Hamilton?' I asked.

'Yes?' There was no recognition in his face. I had not

40

noticed before how pale his lashes were, how pale his eyes.

'Mr Hamilton. I'm Edmund Sin. We met in Monaco. You wanted to meet someone who knew China.' It had sounded reasonable on the train. I wished it still did. 'Here I am.'

'Edmund Sin! Of course I remember now! Your car was stuck, wasn't it? And I guess you must've been the man went to the villa? Mme Vallouris told me about that. What brings you here?'

I thought I had explained, but before I could add anything an ugly man with a handsome moustache spoke: 'This chappie a friend of yours?'

'I guess so, Major,' replied Roscoe Hamilton.

'Shooting chap?' asked the major, offering me his pistol. The answer was no. 'Best give it a try then, what?' he urged.

The gun was obstinately heavy and clumsy in my hand. The mind reacts oddly to unfamiliar situations, I find: instead of concentrating on the target I found myself reviewing what I knew about guns. I had heard of Colt and Westhouse and Winchester, for these were part of the cowboy lore, and knew of other guns too, Lugers and Webleys and Mausers, whose names the War had made familiar. I was just deciding that a Webley sounds like a small furry animal with a pleasant nature, and that being shot by one sounds undignified, when the major spoke. 'What are you waiting for? Just hold it steady . . . squeeze gently . . . gently.' There was a loud crack. My shoulder buckled and bucked. I turned furiously on the major to ask why he had hit me. 'Mind the recoil,' he said through his guffaws.

'Try again,' suggested Roscoe Hamilton.

The second attempt hurt less, but still I did not know where the bullet went.

'Watch.' Roscoe positioned himself next to me, side on to the target, with his legs apart and his back straight. He

41

raised his gun and fired. It was as simple as that. 'Let's go back to the house,' he said. No one demurred: no one checked the bullet had hit the bull. Roscoe could walk on water; he was the pilot who flew with no hands. He collected his cap and jacket and led us out.

We blinked in the high-sided day. Lord Hewcoate introduced himself to me. 'Are you staying in town or would you rather I had a room aired for you?'

'A room would be great. That's very good of you. Thanks.'

'Not at all! Any friend of Roscoe is a friend of mine.' He was speaking rather too loudly; he was speaking for Roscoe to hear. 'I gather you're from China.'

'Sort of,' I conceded.

'My uncle was in Hong Kong only last month. Whereabouts are you from?'

The questioning had begun early. I was resolved to lie as rarely as possible. 'Chicago,' I said.

'Oh? Where the gangsters come from?'

'That's right. Where the gangsters come from. But of course, I know China very well.' Lord Hewcoate was not the only one who spoke loudly for Roscoe to hear.

My luggage had been collected from the hotel, and I changed before going down for dinner. It was the same party as earlier, and I found myself seated between Roscoe and the mustachioed major. 'I gather you're wanting to join Hamilton on his Chinese jaunt?' said the latter as we drank our soup.

'If he'll have me.'

'Let's ask him. Hamilton!' he called, forcing himself between me and my soup plate. 'Are you taking this young fellow to China?'

'It's possible,' replied Roscoe.

The major continued to lean over my soup. 'What for?' he demanded. 'Fellow can't shoot.' There were beads of soup suspended in the handsome moustache. As he laughed, one of them dropped into my soup. I pushed my chair back.

'As a sort of Chingachgook,' replied Roscoe, and again I heard Chicago and did not know what he meant. 'A Chinese–American travelling with me might be useful.'

'As a translator, you mean?'

'Excuse me, sir.' A footman cleared our soup.

'Possibly.' Roscoe was saying, 'But more as a mark of good faith.'

The major snorted, as English majors should. He continued to lean across me as the fish plates were laid. His nose was patterned with broken veins; it was as if the façade of his face were crumbling and the blood was showing through. 'Good faith! I thought it was a hunting trip you were organising, not a bally cultural ensemble!'

Someone else was speaking, the older gentleman who faced me across the table. 'You know, Robbie, that's not the modern attitude.'

The major rounded on him. 'I suppose you're another of those who'd give the Empire away?'

'Not me, Robbie. I was merely remarking that yours isn't the modern attitude.'

'Too many people,' said the major, ignoring the denial, 'lost their nerve in the war. That's what's wrong with this country. Not enough guts to do the job properly.'

'Guts?' asked Lord Hewcoate from the head of the table. 'What are you talking about, Robbie?'

'I'm talking about guts, about courage.'

'I had a better idea about what courage meant before the war.'

'You see?' demanded the major. 'Another one who lost his guts.'

'Of course I lost my guts!' replied our host. 'I had half my bloody stomach shot away!'

I seemed to be the only one who found this funny. 'Sorry, old man,' said the major. 'I forgot.'

'It's all right.'

'I've often wondered,' said Roscoe, 'exactly what courage is. What makes a man act bravely?'

'Defence of something he believes in.'

'Something he loves.'

'Isn't it the need to overcome fear?' suggested the older man opposite. 'Man's always looking to conquer the unknown, but always scared of the unknown. He has to conquer fear before he can achieve anything.'

'Challenge!' interjected the major.

'I suppose so,' said Lord Hewcoate. 'Sometimes it isn't about overcoming fear, it's about *showing* you have overcome fear.'

I was getting interested. I had never given much thought to courage before. Somehow, you always assume you will be brave.

The sixth man spoke for the first time. 'I think of courage like this: curiosity about myself; curiosity about the world.'

'That's because you're a mountaineer. It's different for a soldier.'

The major had started to tell a story. I tried not to listen to him; I wanted to listen to the others. This was a symposium on courage and these men were experts. But the major was hard to ignore. 'Attached to a regiment of native horse,' he said. 'I was owed leave so when Johnnie sent word he was doing a bit of climbing I was glad to join him.'

The other conversation continued around the major. 'To be bored of danger is to be bored of life,' said the mountaineer, refilling his glass. 'In fact, to be bored of danger is to give up life, in my business. Boredom makes you careless.'

'We spent the first few days in the foothills, thoroughly enjoying a bit of strenuous exercise,' said the major.

'Is it danger that makes you hunt big game, Mr Hamilton?'

'A good question,' Roscoe replied. 'I think the major's word, challenge, is better.'

'There was a pinnacle known as the White Arm nearby,' the major was saying, 'and Johnnie asked if I fancied a crack at it.'

'There's the challenge of the organisation, and the challenge of using your own skill, as a tracker and a stalker and a shot. And I guess too there's the challenge of facing the danger if something goes wrong.'

'My feelings exactly,' said the mountaineer.

'But there's more to it than that,' decided Roscoe, thinking aloud by now. 'There's the freedom too. I'm a frontiersman at heart, I reckon.' He smiled.

'After a good day's journey we reached the foot of the pinnacle and set up our tents,' continued the major. 'And the following day began our climb. Johnnie was the more experienced climber and went ahead.'

'A frontiersman? *Last of the Mohicans* stuff?'

Roscoe's self-effacing smile became genuine pleasure.

The major interrupted his story to interrupt us. 'Then this Chinese chappy could be your Mohican.'

'Exactly. My Chicago.'

'Your what?'

'My Chicago. Spelt Chin-gach-gook.'

'Bloody funny way of pronouncing it then,' remarked the major. 'Anyway, the landscape which opened before us now was that of the Moon. Uncountable miles of snowcapped hills stretched away to the higher peaks of the Himalayas. There is nowhere more beautiful in the world.'

'I agree,' said the mountaineer, taking note of the major for the first time.

'As we carried on round the mountain we chanced unexpectedly on a fertile valley running off to the north, completely hidden from the Indian side of the peak.'

I chewed on my steak; English steak takes a lot of

chewing. *'Fortes Fortuna adjuvat,'* said the gentleman opposite. 'Fortune favours the brave.'

'There was a town in the valley, quite a large one. I asked Johnnie where we were. The End of the World was his reply.'

The older man was telling a story too. 'The warrior ran at me,' he said. 'Curious sensation really. I found time to admire every curve of his muscles. I was particularly impressed, I think, by how very bright the highlights were on the muscles of his right arm. He had that arm tensed, you see. That was the arm that held his throwing spear.'

Then I was listening to the major again. 'Below us we could see well dressed natives in uniforms of black and blue, patrolling the jungle paths. "They've seen us!" cried Johnnie, and we turned to run.'

'Valour!' the mountaineer declared. 'That's your word. None of this common-or-garden bravery or courage.' He put his empty glass on the white linen, and caught it as he raised his hand again. 'It's valour I want to see.' A last drop of claret spilt on the cloth.

'What about skill?' asked the older man. 'Bone-headed valour alone is rarely sufficient.'

'They rounded us up and took us back to the town, prodding us all the while with their bayonets. My arms and shoulders were covered with tiny cuts.'

'I had a better idea of what courage meant before the war,' Lord Hewcoate said again.

'They took us to the man I assume was their king. "What's going on?" I asked Johnnie. "I don't know," he replied, "but I'm very much afraid we may have stumbled on Djedun." I'd heard of Djedun, of course, everyone in Assam at the time had. It was the fabled smuggling centre: all the illicit treasures of south-east Asia are said to have passed through there at some time. Opium, precious metals, jewels, slaves. There could be little doubt as to what our fate would be.'

The cheese arrived, and the port, which ended the

conversation but could not stop the major. 'The king spoke English with an Oxford accent. He offered us tiffin. "So pleasant to meet men who are not felons," he told us. "One gets tired of associating exclusively with the criminal classes. It is a shame our acquaintance cannot be prolonged but sadly my sense of duty forbids it." '

'Fine Stilton this,' said the mountaineer. 'You enjoying it, Hamilton?'

'Kind of strong for my taste,' admitted Roscoe. I agreed. Stilton, it seemed, was a mouldy mess smeared into a cheap pot.

'Fine Stilton this,' repeated the moutaineer. 'Even if the Yanks can't appreciate it. Pass round the port, will you?'

'They dragged us to a well in the centre of the square. The men who held us were giants; escape was out of the question. Then the grid over the well was removed and we were forced to stare down into the blackness. "Sorry about this, old chap," said Johnnie but I assured him he wasn't to blame. We started to recite the Lord's Prayer together, but before we could finish it they had thrown him in, and I followed only a second later.

'The next I remember was coming round in the pitch darkness. I couldn't work out what had happened, for I seemed to be still alive. I tried calling, softly, to Johnnie, but there was no reply.

'I had some matches on me. I struck one, and saw at once what had saved my life. I was lying prone on layers of bodies, and these had broken my fall. The people of Djedun must have been holding a lot of executions recently, I decided, for many of these corpses were fresh, and maggots writhed in their flesh. I heard them pop as I moved about. I held the match higher and saw Johnny, but he hadn't shared my incredible luck. His neck was patently snapped.

'I realised of course that I had to escape. There were fouler things than maggots lurking in the layers of human

47

flesh at the foot of the well. I tried to keep calm, to think straight. This was no time to get into a blue funk. You were talking about courage. Courage is controlling your fear, and fear is the sense your body is worth preserving. There's nothing like feeling that you are worth preserving for turning you to jelly or turning you to action. I have never been so frightened and never been so brave.

'I worked out that, whatever it might be now, this charnel house had once been a well and therefore must have contained a water course. Perhaps, therefore, if I dug through the bodies I might reach the water and escape that way. Even if I drowned in the tunnel it would be better than staying to be eaten alive by the maggots and worms. I did not exactly relish the thought of tunnelling throught the corpses, as you can imagine, but I persevered, ignoring the foul and noxious things I grabbed with every handful and concentrating entirely on the thought of survival. Squeamishness was not appropriate.

'I was lucky, as my presence here tonight demonstrates. I reached the tunnel which had carried water to the well, and it was dry. There must have been a cave-in upstream at some time. Slowly, conserving my precious matches, I picked my way along the rubble-strewn floor to freedom.'

The port was warm and sweet. It passed left around the table from Roscoe to me; I took another glass and handed it on to the major. 'Has Hamilton said whether he's going to take you to China yet?'

'Not yet.'

'Come on, Hamilton, make a decision,' said the major. 'I've decided you *should* take this chap along. You said yourself you needed a bit of local colour, and you'll not find a nicer Chink than this.' I don't know what he based this judgement on. 'Look at him. You can see he's a resourceful sort of chappie. Knows China like the back of his hand, he says, and obviously he'll speak the lingo. Though not all the dialects, eh?' He winked at me; I muttered my agreement. 'This, Hamilton, is the sort of fellow a man like you should treasure. Why, I'll bet he can do all manner of things: mix a whisky sour, cure crabs, find a bordello in Perth, get hold of Mary Pickford's telephone number. Isn't that right?' This time his wink was accompanied by a nudge. He nearly winded me.

'You don't need to say anything more,' said Roscoe. 'Edmund's coming along, if he still wants to.'

'I do!' I said.

'Hang on, chappie,' said the major. 'He's not asking you to marry him, you know.'

The party broke up soon after. I went to my room. My mind was full of thoughts of adventure. My mind was full of China. My bladder was full of port wine though, so I made my way to the washroom.

I met the major coming out. He winked again. 'Hope you appreciated that. Knew I could get you on to that expedition if I tried.'

'Thanks very much,' politeness said, though I could not see what he had done for me.

'One thing though,' the major continued. 'Do remember that line about the dialects. You don't want to look an absolute ass when he asks about a spot of translating.' I suppose my face showed my shock; the major grinned. 'When you tell as many tall stories as I do you rather recognise a fib.'

I entered the washroom and locked the door. I thought a bit about the major and then dismissed him. I was young and I was selfish. I thought instead about me.

I was too excited to feel guilt at my deception. All my life so far I had been an observer, and afterwards I was to continue the same way, but just this once I had precipitated myself into the action. I had made things happen and became Chingachgook from Chicago. I liked the symmetry in that: it made me forget the major and the improbity of my position; I was in awe of Roscoe, and I was using him, and instead of feeling bad I felt good.

*

49

We returned to London, where Roscoe had some business. He was trying to arrange support from various zoological functions for his venture: he did not want their money; he wanted their names and respectability. While he was engaged in meetings I looked around the bookshops. I wanted a book that would teach me Chinese. I was out of luck.

The Atlantic liners docked in Liverpool. I wired my father, telling him I had taken a job with Westhouse and hoping all was well at home. I hoped, too, that he would not mind me leaving my studies, but I kept that out of the telegram. I sent on my address: the *Mauretania* for the next few days, and afterwards the Astoria, New York.

It rained as we left England. Liverpool was edged with warehouses, and the backstreets peered through a drizzle of lace curtains at a cold grey world. The *Mauretania* steamed from the port, vibrating calmly. Roscoe and I stood on the deck. 'It's good to be on the move again,' he told me.

We smoked a cigarette and then went inside, down a panelled corridor to the saloon. 'You'll have a drink?' he asked.

'A dry martini, thank you.'

'Dry martini,' he ordered, 'and an orange squash for me.' He gave his name for the check but the barman tut-tutted indulgently: everyone aboard knew Mr Hamilton.

We raised our glasses. 'I guess a toast is in order,' said Roscoe. 'To pandas.'

'Pandas,' I echoed, and our glasses kissed.

NEW WORLD

4
New York

I did not sleep well last night but, in the intervals of calm
between the shiver and sweat of being awake, I had a
delicate, compelling dream. I dreamt of New York.
Generally, if there is one consistent factor in the incon-
stancy of my dreams, it is that architecture is exaggerated.
This modest Monte Carlo apartment grows huge as I
sleep; my father's Lake Shore Drive house becomes a
mansion of many rooms. But when I dreamt of New York
it was unchanged. New York is already exaggerated.

It was a silent and rather lovely dream. Manhattan's
towers were rose tinted by the morning sun, and their
windows flashed messages, flashed fire. I sailed along
East River, beneath the Brooklyn Bridge, and the water
was black and gold. Cars, their headlamps blazing, passed
rhythmically overhead. When I awoke there was a highway bored through my heart, and I was sick for home.

Trans-Atlantic liners always dock on the Hudson, however, so I never made that voyage up the East River; we
docked in the shadow of the Woolworth Building, and a
limousine collected us from the ship.

We were taken to the Astoria. I had not stayed there
before. It was as plump and old-fashioned as its furniture;
even the guests were over-stuffed.

The following morning a message came for Roscoe,
from Washington. The President was hoping to see Mr
Hamilton before he left for China. An airplane was
available. 'Sorry to leave you,' he said. 'But I can't refuse
this. I'll be away at least a week. Why don't you stay here,

go to the museum, see what you can find out?'

I was aiming for the American Museum of Natural History, which was giving scientific sponsorship to Roscoe's expedition. My aim has never been good though. On the way I met George Mulligan. George and I had roomed together at college. We went to Bustonby's and had cocktails all the afternoon.

George worked in advertising. He was broke in the prosperous Twenties; in the Thirties, while the rest of us languished in Hard Times, George became a millionaire. He died in 1938, of too much work and liquor. He had the biggest collection of Race Records, jazz for a negro audience, I have ever known. I have often wondered where those records went.

'Why'n't you come and stay with me? Alice won't mind; Alice ain't home.'

'Who's Alice?'

'My wife. She's left me.'

He lived in Greenwich Village. We took the elevated railway. 'You wouldn't mind going ahead of me half a block or so?' he asked. His voice was always more Irish when it was required to make requests.

'Sure. Why?'

'Somebody I want to avoid,' he said. 'A little debt.'

He gave me the key and the address. 'If anyone asks, I've gone away and you're letting my place for a week or two. No: better make it a month.'

I walked away from him. The streets of the Village are crazy after the rest of New York, as if the blueprint got crushed and no one bothered to straighten it. When I got to the door of George's there was someone waiting.

'You know Mulligan?' I was asked as I tried the key.

'He's away for a month. I've let this place.'

'A month, huh?' The man had an Italian accent and a scar. He had left the violin case in his roadster. 'If you see Mulligan, tell him Luigi wants him. Okay?'

'Sure. Luigi wants him.'

54

'Dat's right. You just tell him good.'

The Italian went. I looked round but could see no sign of George. What the hell, I thought, and let myself in.

He arrived an hour later. He was not alone. The bell rang and when I opened the door I found George supported between Luigi and Luigi's older, meaner, brother. 'You'd better get packing,' Luigi said to me. 'Mr Mulligan ain't going no place for a month after all.'

They shoved George at me. He looked terrible. His eye was split and so was his lip. 'See you round,' said Luigi. I closed the door.

'Are you all right?' I asked, which was a pretty dumb thing to say.

George thought so too. 'Of course I'm not. Fix me a drink!'

'What have you been doing?'

'I told you, it's just a little debt. Don't worry about it. It's all sorted out anyway; Luigi's all right, he's a friend.' What did that make me? 'Forget him: make yourself at home. If the water's off, don't worry. I've been having kind of a rough time with the amenities. The electricity sometimes goes as well, but that gives us an excuse to get out.'

'How much do you need?'

He put his hat back on. 'I said forget it. Keep your dough to buy the hooch,' he said, and we went out.

We went uptown. George explained through his busted lip that these fashionable places, Bustonby's or Shanley's or Jack's, were all very well, but for real jazz you went to a real dive. He took me to a speakeasy where the jazz was good and the liquor raw. Bootlegged gin was made from United States Inspected pure grain alcohol, intended for the cleaning of surgical instruments; they added distilled water, juniper juice and, if you were lucky, a laxative to prevent any permanent harm. The singer had to sing the tables: an amplified voice might be heard outside. George got memorably drunk that night. It must have been memorable. It is all I remember.

The days went by. Roscoe wrote, care of the Astoria, to tell me he would be delayed in Washington until the beginning of September, another two weeks at least. I gave up my rooms and moved in with George.

George worked irregular hours, afternoons mostly, and until I tired of the constant noise of his various creditors I used to stay in and improve my knowledge of China. After two days I had endured enough. I started walking: I gawped at the Chariot Race sign and the Battery like every other rubber-necker, and in the evenings I drank. Everyone drank. Because liquor was limited by law, people stopped limiting it by sense. We drank until we had to stop, and at every chance we drank too much.

I met Cecelia Frayle one day outside Macy's. I had known her in Chicago, when she had been Cecelia Magenbraun. Everyone had predicted she would make a brilliant marriage. She had not let them down.

'I love your husband's books,' I told her. *A Butterfly of Passion* had made him into a celebrity; *The Angels' Wings* into a prophet. He was a seer for a Lost Generation, like Scott Fitzgerald, or Michael Arlen in England; like them, he treated our petty concerns and unexpected affluence as if they were real.

'You must come to our party!' she said, for this was the era of parties.

'Sure,' I replied. 'I'd love to.'

I arrived at the party on time, which was too early. A coloured maid opened the door. 'Mr Frayle isn't in.'

'Mrs Frayle invited me to a party,' I explained. I offered her Cecelia's calling card; it had the date hand-written on the back.

'Mr Frayle is out rounding folks up right now.'

'Is Mrs Frayle in?'

'She's fixing herself up.'

'Can I wait?'

She let me in reluctantly, taking the card from me like it was a ticket. I thought she might tear it in half.

It was a fine apartment. A team of caterers was busily organising the food. The maid indicated I should stay out of their way so I walked out on the balcony. We were seven storeys up, and to the right Central Park was green between the white buildings. The sun had just gone and the sky was pale.

The maid came back. 'Mrs Frayle will be out any moment. You didn't give your name.'

'I'm Edmund Sin.'

To my surprise she smiled. 'Really?'

I smiled back. We were no longer enemies. 'Really.'

'I'll fix you a drink.'

'It doesn't matter.'

'Mrs Frayle said I should.'

'All right. I'll have a manhattan.' It seemed appropriate.

'Sin!' she said. 'That sure is some name!'

A group of the caterers came through lugging a cake the shape of a skyscraper. The maid told them which table to put it on while a man in a dark shirt and a light tie delivered bottles by the case. I sipped my manhattan and waited.

Cecelia entered the room. 'Edmund!' she said, ravishing in organdie. 'I'm so glad you could make it!'

She said it as if she meant it and led me to the balcony. We looked down on to East 68th where the trapped traffic jostled. 'What brings you to New York?' she asked. 'I heard you were in Paris.'

'I've gotten a job,' I explained. 'With Roscoe Hamilton.'

'The big-game hunter?'

'Yes. We're going to China to hunt a big bear called a Giant Panda.'

'I've read about that,' said Cecelia. 'I didn't know Roscoe Hamilton was going though. I thought it was just the Roosevelt brothers.'

'The Roosevelt brothers?'

'Teddy and Kermit. It's been in all the papers. Hadn't you heard?'

'No,' I admitted, puzzled.

'What sort of job have you gotten, anyhow? I don't see you as a big-game hunter, Edmund. You're more of an indoors man.'

'I'm Roscoe's Chingachgook,' I said proudly, but I pronounced it Chicago and she looked confused.

The apartment door opened that moment and we heard a score of voices in the lobby. 'My husband,' muttered Cecelia. We came in off the balcony to receive her guests.

'Let me through!' cried a voice from the crowd. 'There's been an accident! Let me through! I'm an attorney!' A small good-looking man in a white tuxedo, his arms round a bob-headed girl, came up to Cecelia and gave her a kiss. 'Hi!'

'Lawton,' she said formally. 'This is Edmund Sin, a friend from Chicago.'

'I've read your books,' I said. He smiled at me pleasantly and then announced to the people following him that they should leave their clothes in the bedroom. There was laughter at this, and more laughter as they made their way through.

Cecelia looked at her husband, who was abandoned now in the middle of the room. 'You've had too much again,' she said.

'Don't start.'

'I'm not starting anything.'

'Then what would you call it?'

'A statement of fact. I simply made a statement of fact.'

'You make me sick.'

The guests returned, as noisily as they had gone. A different languid girl embraced Frayle. Cecelia did not bother to look at me; I did not want to look at her.

Guests kept arriving; the room was filling up. The Frayles formed two distinct groups. He perched on a table, talking loudly and well, while she sat on a sofa surrounded by men.

I met some people from Chicago. They had come up on the Twentieth Century specially for Cecelia's party. 'She hasn't changed a bit,' they said, and I wished that this were true.

Frayle was magnificent that evening. I had no intention of liking him, and no reason for respecting him, yet as he gave his address on the State of the Union I found myself doing both. 'Some people claim the force behind the American people is enterprise. They see Henry Ford and John Hamilton and believe it when they read that "What's good for General Motors is good for America". Others, more cynically, hold that the main motive we all share is cupidity, the love of money. But I know different. I've been doing some journalism in Florida and my conclusion, based on what I discovered Down South, is that the overriding characteristic of the American people is that they're nuts.'

People laughed. Someone pointed out that what applied to Dixieland need not apply to New Jersey. 'You'd deny it?' demanded Frayle. 'Then I'll prove it.

'First, a definition of lunacy. A lunatic, we'd all agree, is someone who confuses what's real and what's imagined. Now, I first went to Miami a couple of years back. The place was teeming with real-estate agents. There were two thousand offices and twenty-five thousand agents in Miami alone: the city fathers had to pass a law to stop sales being made in the street as the wheeler-dealing was blocking the traffic. And Miami was just one spot along the coast. All Florida was the same. Miami's population grew in a few years from thirty thousand to a hundred and fifty thousand, and those who couldn't get there in person sent their money on instead and bought up land.

'Not that they were actually paying cash for their real estate. Oh no! They put down a deposit of ten per cent and owed the rest. It didn't matter because they could always sell the land at a profit if funds got tight: land values were doubling every few months at the height of the boom; fifty by a hundred feet areas of Florida might change hands forty times in as many weeks, and at a profit every time. A paper profit, that is. No one actually cared about the quality of the land itself, of course. No one cared that there were no utilities, no drainage, no buildings being completed. All they cared was that they had invested in Paradise, and no one could ever make a bum deal in Paradise.

'But suddenly, last summer, not so many people were interested in Paradise. The ballyhoo was dying down, and what was left looked like a building lot. People started worrying about the ninety per cent on each investment they owed and *hadn't* paid, and started pushing for the balance of the money that they were owed on the resale. Just imagine a piece of property selling at ten thousand dollars. Forget the real-estate agents' cuts and the fact that most people made a good profit. Just imagine that ten people have, in the course of a year, bought and then sold that land. Each has put down ten per cent, one thousand, and owes nine thousand, but the debt doesn't worry him because he's resold and the resale has brought in the one thousand in cash and the promise of another nine thousand. There was no danger, so long as no one defaulted.

'Last year, people defaulted. September 18, 1926: eleven months back, and while the punters were staying away from Florida that year, the hurricanes weren't. The second hurricane of the season hit that day and carried a five-masted schooner the length of Coral Gables, depositing it right outside City Hall.

'The people who had gotten rid of their land breathed a sigh of relief, of course – until they discovered a whole chain of people ahead of them clamouring for their ninety per cents. For every piece of land, ten, twenty, fifty people were going under. The whole state failed: Paradise went bust. The bougainvillaea and the Chinese Alphabet plants blossomed again in the water-logged foundations, and the alligators wept crocodile tears.

'I'm going to write a story about this; I've got to write a story about this. How the American people bought a share of Paradise. It's going to be called *Paradise Retailed*.'

We laughed, but someone had an objection. 'All right, we're dreamers. It doesn't make us mad.'

Frayle raised an elegant eyebrow. 'No?'

'What's wrong with chasing a dream?' He looked around for support. 'That's what made America what it is.'

Frayle thought carefully before speaking. 'You're right,' he said. 'Chasing a dream made America what it is. I feel prophetic tonight. Last year saw the collapse of a single state; next year, or the year after, we'll see the collapse of the whole Union.'

'Come on, Lawton. Let's go down Coney Island,' said a man I thought I recognised as Al Krager, the painter.

Frayle continued urbanely. 'Pleasure must wait on prophecy. The insanity of America runs deep. It isn't only the gullible, the certifiable, the reprehensible who suffer. You don't have to act the village idiot to be mad. It's in every one of us, in our institutions, in our Constitution. And why not? Aren't we all descended from dream-chasers? Isn't our friend here right when he claims America was built on a dream? Our ancestors gave up the certainty of the tangible for the promise of a dream when they left Europe for America. Is it so surprising that we live in a nation characterised by its lunacy? Is it so surprising we should all be mad? Let's go for that drive. Let's prove

61

we're mad. Let's jump off Brooklyn Bridge.'

We left together, about fifteen of us, and as I left I passed Cecelia, surrounded by her beaux. She saw I was going with her husband and turned away.

We went to a funfair and it was closed. We drove down an alley. The skeletal dipper reared up behind a bleached wood hoarding. Overhead the elevated railway splashed the pylons with light, and our headlamps found fire hydrants and trash cans. Frayle jumped from his convertible and stood with his back against the wall, pinned in the headlamps' beams. 'Consider this,' he said. 'According to Sophocles there were no witnesses to Oedipus's death. All that is known is that he travelled across the seas, west to the Happy Isles. And we all know where that must be.

'Unfortunately, like all immigrants, Oedipus had to wait on Ellis Island before being admitted here, and the immigration authorities were doubtless a little sceptical about allowing in a blind, lame, incestuous old man. United States' statutes are very strict. They prohibit paupers, polygamists, prostitutes and anarchists; they also prohibit – to illustrate what an up-to-date nation this is – people with inferiority complexes! Which means by the way that all our paupers, polygamists, prostitutes and anarchists must be entirely home grown.

'To check Oedipus's credentials they asked him a question. What rides on three wheels in the morning, seventy-two in the afternoon, and four in the evening? To which the wily Greek replied Man, who rides a tricycle as a kid, a suburban railroad car as a man, and is driven to the grave in a motorised hearse. So the immigration people were forced to admit him, although, according to their quaint custom, they first Anglicised his name. Oedipus became Ed Opus.

'He found accommodation on the Greek tenements in Lower East, a block of railroad flats with the rooms strung end to end and the only light coming from the filthy stairwell. All around him people were following his example and plucking out their eyes to avoid seeing reality, and pouring out their miseries to this distinguished and wise old man, until Oedipus could stand the sufferings no longer. "Enough! I shall avenge myself on the Founding Fathers!" he cried. Fathers, after all, were his speciality.

'He traced them to the ballroom of the Astoria. The first he dispatched quickly with a blow to the neck which drove the poor man's spine through his flesh. The second took rather longer because our hero split several of his veins and let him bleed. A third cowered in the corner mumbling Plymouth prayers, which so infuriated Oedipus that he ripped the man's jaw off and let him drown in his own blood. And the fourth . . . the fourth . . . and the fourth.'

'It's time we were getting back,' said Al Krager, walking over to Frayle.

'Sure,' Frayle replied. 'Lend me your coat, will you? I'm kind of cold.'

It was almost dawn when we arrived back at the apartment. We took the elevator and waited in the corridor while Frayle let himself in. 'Shhh!'

The block was silent; the party over. Frayle took off his shoes and entered the apartment like a vaudeville villain. We giggled as we followed. He turned on the light. 'Drink!' he decided.

A door opened. Cecelia stepped out. She still wore her party dress but her face, stripped of make-up, was tired and drawn. One of the saddest things I know is when a lovely woman is ugly and does not care.

Frayle spoke first. 'Good morning, honey.'

She looked at him blankly as if the words made no sense. I saw how tight she held her lower lip. 'Get out,' she said.

He was at a disadvantage with his shoes still in his hand. He put them down.

'I said "Get out"!'

Slowly he straightened. 'Don't be unreasonable, sweetheart.'

'Just get out!'

'Christ.'

'Damn you!'

'Please!'

'Just go! All of you! All of you just get out now!' She was crying now. The last dregs of the mascara she had been unable to clean now washed down her cheeks in lines of grime. 'Just get out. Please.'

'Cecelia!' He stepped forward and she stepped back. 'Don't touch me,' she warned.

He took another step. 'Cecelia!'

'Keep away.' She was wary, hunted; he circled her like a fighter. She backed against the skyscraper cake and he followed.

'Cecelia!'

'Keep away!'

'Cecelia!'

'No!'

'Cecelia!'

He lunged forward heavily, knocking the skyscraper to the floor, tier after tier falling in on itself and sliding inelegantly into the carpet. Cecelia screamed. She ran out on to the balcony and we followed like a pack.

The sun was up now, climbing through an early fog. I found myself next to Frayle at the balcony door. 'What do I do?' he asked, and I thought he was asking me.

The daylight put some colour in her face. She shook her head. We watched her turn at the balustrade, and lean her weight, and fall. Her perfect silk dress blossomed and bloomed, and then she was broken and strange on the sidewalk, and the beautiful organdie silk became something the tide had washed in.

64

Frayle sobbed and stepped forward. I thought he would jump too, so I held his arm and he did not resist. 'Cecelia!' he said, as he had said it so many times, and then louder, wailing, '*Cecelia*'! His sobs shook him a few times and then he was silent and still. I let my hand fall from his sleeve as he straightened his back. 'She was unbalanced,' he said, and I almost laughed at the desperate ambiguity. 'There was nothing I could have done.'

I looked at him. He had made his decision: there was nothing he could have done. I looked at him. I felt nausea then, and contempt.

Even the police are expensive in that part of Manhattan. We gave our statements and were allowed home. No one, guests or police, mentioned the empty bottles. I travelled back on the el., wondering what I ought to be thinking. Death is beyond our thoughts: it defines us yet we cannot define it.

Sometimes I think she jumped for him, that she did it because he was a novelist and his imagination demanded it. Sometimes I think she did it for herself, because she dramatised herself and loved to make beautiful sad gestures.

And sometimes, when I think of the image of a lovely woman plunging to the gutter, and think of Lindbergh and Wall Street and Roscoe and Al Capone, I think she did it for America and for our dreams.

5

Harlem

After Cecelia's death George was very concerned for me. He wanted to take me somewhere special where we could hear good jazz and talk things through. George was a great believer in talking things through. Most of his problems came that way.

We began the night at the Cotton Club, where Adelaide Hall sang 'Creole Love Call'. I enjoyed it and would happily have stayed but George was critical. 'Cosmetic black, black-face black,' he called it. 'We're looking for the real thing. Some orgiastic piano-stomping party where the music will sing your heart out.'

We went north, into Harlem, and we went on foot because George wanted to hear any music in the air. It had been a hot day. Pools of water, filmed with dust, gathered where the hydrants had been opened. We passed an old negro selling yams fried in dough, his stove straddling the sidewalk edge. The stovepipe trailed an oily smoke, and for a moment the air was full of a sweet and alien scent. There were children still out on the street, though it was late, and we could hear their rhymes.

The sidewalks were shadowed, the alleys worse. There were stars above us, seen vaguely through the uptown haze, but they cast no light. We found ourselves walking the middle of the street like gunfighters. George talked bravely about a woman he had never known.

'Suicide,' he said, treasuring the word. 'Suicide. Like Whitman says, "Come lovely and soothing death." Whitman knew about death, I reckon. He knew about death and that's how he knew about life.' He knew even more about death now, I thought, but said nothing. George would have ignored me anyhow. 'We all want to be enfolded in death's pale and languid arms. That's Whitman's message. Death is a lovely woman. They used to call orgasm "the little death". I guess that makes death the big orgasm, the earth-shattering sneeze. And when you sneeze they say your heart stops. It does when you ejaculate too. Imagine that: you're spreading your seed, starting a new life, and just at the moment it bursts out of you in a spurt, your heart stops!'

He had always talked like this. There was nothing to be done but listen. Sometimes it was good to listen, but that night I was nervous. 'What might Whiman have made of tonight?' he asked rhetorically. There was a lot of rhetoric in George. 'A gently rocking cradle on a breeze that's tainted with yams, while the city of dust is hustling in the sidewalk and the alleys are full of poor kids without shoes, whose naked tootsies in the gutter are stretched to catch anything valuable washed downstream from the fire hydrants' illicit gush? Is that what he would have seen? Slavery's innocent victims chucking coins on the street corners? Maimed to the fifth generation, the Africans blowing their horns in the dark? "The foulest crime in history", Whitman called slavery, and by God he was right. What would he have made of tonight?'

'I don't know,' I replied. 'Where are we going?'

'Always so practical. Anyplace and everyplace is our destination.' Cotton Club champagne came at thirty dollars a bottle and George was determined to savour what he could of this expensive sensation. 'The world is our oyster.'

'Okay. So now tell me where we're going.'

'I have done!' He sounded surprised. 'Weren't you listening?'

'Yes, but . . . '

'We're there! We're listening now for the sound of a horn moaning on the streets, the shuffle of a piano's bass

67

maybe, or a wailing saxophone haunting the alley-
ways.'

'We're not going anywhere specific then?'

'What could be more specific than this?' He waved both
arms at the wide street and the dingy buildings; he was
beginning to draw attention to us. 'We are listening for
the sweet call of jazz. These are the horns that brought
down Jericho. In a thousand plantation nights, honed on
the rhythms of their past, the black Americans have found
once more the exact and destructive tones first used by
Joshua. Alleluia! In the flattened third and the flattened
seventh of the blue-note scale lie the keys of the Promised
Land, where the Horn of Plenty will be swinging in the
streets. Listen for the cornucopia of jazz! Listen, oh
doubter, and learn!'

'George,' I cautioned.

'What is it?' He sounded annoyed at the interruption,
but at least he dropped his voice.

'I want to know where we are going. Or rather, now I
know, I want to go back.'

'Are you yellow?'

'Yes. I am.'

He looked at me and laughed. 'By God you are! And
I'm a mad Irishman whose father, God rest his soul, made
it from the waterfront to Congress on the strength of the
sublime gift of words. Fear not, young mate-of-my-soul,
though you be a heathen Chinese on the outside, the mad
luck of the Mulligans is upon you and shall remain with
you for ever and ever ah-men.'

A crowd was gathering. The children had followed us
first, cake-walking behind us provocatively. George did
not care: he took off his bow-tie and tossed it to them; a
little girl tied it in her hair. Now certain local toughs were
behind us, rolling their shoulders and hips as they walked.
'Keep your voice down,' I muttered. 'We're attracting
attention.'

'Nonsense. Silence would be a betrayal of the holy

principles of jazz.' His voice was quieter though, despite his words, and the crowd around us grew. Women followed now, fat ones who had come from doorways and thin ones who lurked in alleys. We were becoming a parade. 'My people,' said George, awed. 'My beautiful people.' He took off his jacket and slung it over his shoulder. A young man brought out a trumpet and played it as we walked, blowing a mocking 'Yankee-DoodleDandy' up-register and bending the notes in the runs. George was delighted. 'We haven't found a party,' he said. 'We *are* the party.'

We stopped walking. Despite the geometrical grid of Manhattan I was lost. I felt I had never been this far north, or this far south. There were nearly thirty people in the street with us now, and others watching from the steps and the alleys. The yam salesman had followed the crowd: the flavour of his fruit still softened the city air. George and I found ourselves backing against the dubious security of his portable stove, which was built on the chassis of an old baby carriage. The trumpeter stopped playing. The sudden silence was a threat.

George was full of bravado or misplaced bonhomie. 'Friends!' he cried. 'How do you do?'

A young tough approached, and the crowd settled around us in a semi-circle. The tough drew a flick-knife and held it loosely in his hand, the blade still sheathed. Quickly he turned on George; the blade erupted in the space between them. The tough grinned politely, and used it to pick his teeth. 'What you doing here?'

'Just walking.' George's confidence had become bluster and the tough, realising this, spat efficiently into the street.

'Scram,' he said. He made it a curse.

'We can walk here if we like,' said George, falling back on his rights.

'Mister,' said the negro. 'You cain't.' He folded his flick-blade away. The tension went with the knife. The confrontation was over and already the crowd was losing interest.

George lifted his head. 'Come on Edmund. We're clearly not wanted here.'

'You like a yam, mister?' asked the salesman. 'No charge. You's been worth a fortune to me, damn right.'

George, his face set, walked on by.

In time we reached different streets, where the shops had Jewish names and police patrols patrolled. 'I just don't get that attitude,' said George when we were well clear. 'Why wouldn't they let us be there? Don't they want our help?'

I was silent. I was thinking. Poor George, I was thinking, who had blustered in with his white man's confidence and expected Harlem to be grateful. His was the missionary spirit: he handed over a white god and a white message and was puzzled when he cooked in a big black pot.

'Edmund,' he said. 'I don't want to be offensive, but do you think it was because you were with me? Perhaps it was that they didn't like.'

I could not reply. I was hurt by his words, and I was hurt he might be right.

The next day I moved back to the Astoria and asked for news of Roscoe. He was due back that very afternoon. There was also a letter for me. I took it, and recognised my mother's writing, which surprised me. It was always my father who wrote.

Father was ill, she said, and she wanted me home. I sat down in the foyer and wondered what to do. Half my mind was frightened for my father; the other half feared Roscoe would go to China without me now. I decided to wait for Roscoe before I left New York. Half a day could make no difference: the letter was already four days old.

He arrived in a flurry of under-managers, who wrung their hands and hoped he had been well. I was flattered by the way he ignored them and greeted me. 'Edmund!' he said. 'How are you?'

I showed him the letter. 'Is he bad?' he asked when he had read it.

'Mother wouldn't write me if he wasn't.'

'Take the Twentieth Century. I'd get you an airplane but I don't think it would be any quicker. You can use my name when you get the ticket. Or better still I'll book it for you.' He called for a telephone line to Grand Central. 'I've pretty well finished here in the East. The next stop is Hollywood; I want to take a camera crew along. You can join me there. I guess you'll have heard by now that the Roosevelt brothers are setting up in opposition.' I told him I had. 'It's a race. Which reminds me, you'd better get off to the station. I hope everything goes all right for you.'

'Thank you.'

'Give my best wishes to your dad, too.' He paused. 'You care about your father, don't you.'

I was surprised this needed saying. 'Yes.'

'That's good,' he said. 'That's very good. You ought to be on your way now. The train won't wait.'

I took a cab. New York Central seemed especially vast, especially lonely, that afternoon: a cathedral full of the incense of wood-smoke and coal. I had a quarter of an hour so I visited the can. The water closets' wooden lids were like eye-patches. I felt the rich lean smell of urine and the fat mean smell of cleansing agent wrap round me. There were shiny black tubes exposed on the walls, and the urinals were like the hollowed backs of sculpted women. No one spoke. Everyone there was a transient.

It was the days before locomotives got really lovely; in 1927 they were still pipes and tubes and hissing leaks, raw as something turned inside out. They were fine to look at though, long and lean and hungry, cowboys herding the bovine cars out of the city. My train, the Twentieth Century Limited, was waiting and I climbed

71

aboard. This was the train that would take me home.

Now it is a different September. Monaco is quieter after the summer rush and the races, and I am a confirmed exile. Then I had not seen Chicago in a year; now I have not been back in seven, and though Senator McCarthy is dead, and America has a new President, I do not think I shall be returning there just yet. *Are you now, or have you ever been, a member of the Communist Party?* I shall not be returning just yet.

I never faced the committee; I was never asked the infamous question. Sometimes I wish I had been interrogated. I could have vented my frustration.

I had been doing all right, doing swell. My column was syndicated to thirty-one states. I had a network of contacts in government. And then I was blacklisted.

Seventy-six newspapers coast-to-coast had used my column, and suddenly I could not get a byline in the *Farson County Weekly Gleaner*. For a while I kept going on the stories I could sell abroad, but soon there were no stories left to tell. My sources dried up. There are many reasons people talk to a columnist: malice, intolerance, duty; envy, failure, love. The one thing they have in common is they want their story heard. A reporter who cannot get printed is a jockey without a horse.

In the end I retired. I was in my fifties and so was the century: despite my track record editors in Europe or Australia were hardly going to be queuing for my services. We moved to Canada for a year, but that did not work. Monaco was my wife's idea: I was in a maudlin, lethargic mood and it did not seem to matter much where I was; I had been blacklisted and I could no longer write. Then came my wife's cancer, and as she grew weaker I grew stronger, which is often the way even when we love. And then she died.

Are you now, or have you ever been, a member of the Communist Party?

I have spent many years planning my replies.

Are you now, or have you ever been, a member of the Communist Party?

I would speak low; they would not hear.

Speak up, Mr Sin. I'm sure we would all like to know your answer.

So I would speak up. Do you see me? I'm Chinese. And there is an old saying amongst my people which could be translated as 'No, but who gives a damn for the truth?' The truth is irrelevant here. You've seen me. You know that I'm yellow and I'm red and you can bet I love the blacks. That's what you've decided, isn't it Senator? Oh, and Senator, perhaps you'd like to learn that old saying I was talking about? You would? That's great. You see, I may look Chinese but I don't speak much of the language; I'm from Chicago, and the phrase my people would use is Fuck You.

Today our President is an Irish Catholic with a taste for display. I never got to know Jack Kennedy, though I knew his brother Joe before he died in the war. Everyone who knew him tipped Joe for the Presidency; young Jack slipped in as first reserve. Until April 1961 I had thought Jack Kennedy was going to be all right. He was good on Civil Rights. He knew the right people. My wife and I had even talked of returning to the States. And then, on April 17, 1961, a man called José Cardona led fifteen hundred Cuban exiles ashore at the Bay of Pigs, and we decided to stay in Europe.

And yet, and yet. Kennedy *is* good on human rights. Maybe I should return. I shall finish this story by the birthday I share with Voltaire, and then we shall see. An old newshound like me needs his deadlines, and what is more dead than the past. I guess I should like to die in the States; I should like to be going home.

Going home. The Twentieth Century travelled northwest, moving from smudged New Jersey suburbs into the white farmsteads of the Great Lakes. These were the Prohibition states, the dry states, and it began to rain. I saw farmhouses and verandahs and comfortable wide fields through a layer of water on the windows. Fall had begun.

Pennsylvania, Ohio, Indiana, Illinois. We passed Lake Superior, flat and grey.The locomotive shimmered past the lake. The lake met up with the sky.

We must be in Ohio by now, I decided. I thought of Sherwood Anderson's great short stories, and of Warren Harding, who was from Marion, Ohio: he had been a small-town politician who had made it to the White House, and whilst President he had carried on like a provincial town boss, giving privileges to his old Marion cronies, 'The Ohio Gang', who sold off presidential favours at a price reckoned to be somewhere between thirty pieces of silver and a mess of potage. Roscoe's father, Calvin, had been one of Harding's cronies, and I thought about the photograph of Harding in Roscoe's trophy room. It was better to think of Roscoe's father; it was better than thinking about my father, my father's illness.

Harding was a topical issue in the fall of 1927, although he had been dead four years: investigations were continually uncovering fresh scandals about his administration, and the Teapot Dome issue looked like being the juiciest of all.

Does anyone remember Teapot Dome any more? It was the great *cause célèbre* of the day, and as it intrudes into this story again maybe I ought to sketch the essential facts. Teapot Dome was a Naval Oil Reserve. In the Twenties it had been correctly worked out that the biggest naval threat was posed by Japan, and it was agreed that to counter that threat the Navy should have its own indigenous oil reserves, which would be independent of commercial interests. It was a farsighted programme, but there was a problem: while gushers may be easy to spot, the subterranean extent of an oil field is harder to chart. The Navy's oil-bearing reserves neighboured other people's wells; the other people were busy pumping. It seemed likely that the Naval Oil Reserves were being drained by their neighbours, so it was decided the only way to counter this was for the Navy to drill the oil itself. The Navy had little experience in these matters however, so control of the operation was handed over to Harding's Secretary of the Interior, Albert B. Fall. Fall's solution to the problem of what to do with the Naval Oil Reserves was to contract out the leases on the oil fields: the Mammoth Oil Company won the Teapot Dome contract, and drilling began.

Not quite as satisfactory as the government's original scheme, perhaps, but all fairly straightforward. Except that Fall used the cover of National Security to keep quiet about the whole affair, and meantime bonds in a mysterious Canadian company controlled by the directors of the Mammoth Oil Company kept turning up in odd places. Some seemed to be securing loans to Albert B. Fall; there were others apparently sitting in the Republican party's coffers.

It was developing into a messy and comprehensive scandal. Harding's standing had been high at the time of his death, but by 1927 his reputation was as corrupt as his corpse. That very month his mistress, Nan Britton, had published a volume of memoirs that finally and irrevocably smeared the former President. It was often said that it was a good thing for everyone that Harding had died when he did.

I looked out the window. We were almost there: Michigan was a flat white horizon ahead. The sun was low and the shadow of our train raced to keep up, careering recklessly over the obstacles and into the gullies. I thought of Roscoe, and of me.

Outside now were the shacks and hobo camps that were always the first sign of Chicago. Stubbed-out off-white tents crumpled like cigarette butts on the grey ash between the tracks, and smouldered a miserly smoke. I had arrived.

6
Chicago

The air was cold, sweeping down unhindered from the Arctic, and shadows that had been firm in August were slushy in late September. The derelicts who slept under Michigan Avenue Bridge lit fires of stockmarket ticker-tape to keep out the cold, and in the stockyards and slaughterhouses the hands of the workers were as raw, chopped and lifeless as meat.

It was early evening when I arrived. The boomtime brokers on La Salle were counting the day's profits, the South Side brothels hung out red lights, the pigeons roosted in Maxwell Street, and in the police station on Forty-eighth Precinct patrolmen unbuckled their guns and shared out their graft. I got a cab. Chicago is a lovely word for an ugly town.

The cabbie called me Mac. He talked all the time. He told me of this hood called Hymie Vice. I guess we were talking about Hymie Weiss, gunned down in front of O'Banion's flower-shop the year before. 'He was a good customer but a real bad guy. He used to ask for me special. I was the one took him the day he got rubbed out.'

My parents' house was in a wooded suburb north-west of the town. Mary, the parlourmaid, opened the door for me; her husband Nat fetched my cases. They were more deferential than I remembered: was this because I was getting older, or because my father was?

'The doctor's with him right now,' said Mary. 'Your mother too.'

'Is he all right?' There was no answer for her to give.

77

I wanted a drink but my father would have none in the house. We are Americans, he used to say: we obey the law. I took off my hat and coat and climbed the stairs. Half-way up I passed a window and looked out. From inside the house the night was black. It had begun to sleet. Thick damp smears ran down the glass, as unpleasant and slow as phlegm.

Outside the door of my father's room I stopped and straightened my tie. I knocked gently and opened the door. The room was as I had imagined, darkened as if with concern. The doctor and my mother sat each side of the big bed, framing the sick man heraldically. There were odours in the stuffy room, bed baths and sickness and disinfectant, senile smells I did not associate with my father. I closed the door gently behind me, and as it clicked shut the doctor and my mother drew back from the bed. They looked furtive: they were guilty of grief and of knowing my father would die.

'Hello, Mother,' I said softly. 'Dr Hendrix.'

There was a pause I could no nothing about. 'Your father has had a stroke,' said my mother at last. It sounded like a prepared statement, and it probably was.

'Oh.' I stood by the door as if I might flee. 'May I . . . '

'Sure,' said the doctor, and I approached the bed.

There was a stranger lying there. His mouth was collapsed to the left, dragged down in a scowl. His cheek slopped loosely against the jowls, and its weight stretched open an eye. The other side of his face was asleep. Its eye was closed. I could not weep for the destroyed left-hand side of his face, but for the right side, which was still the face of my father, I felt I could scream. I turned to my mother. I was tense with emotion. She held out her arms for me and, uncharacteristically, we embraced.

'I'll wait downstairs,' said the doctor.

We stepped back from one another. I looked again at my father, and saw his sightless eye watch an infinity of space. There are two kinds of dark: there is the darkness that hems you in, suffocating every pore; and there is the other, the empty dark, the one that goes on for ever. Death is both kinds of dark, and my father was almost there.

'I'll see the doctor off,' said Mother.

'I'll come too.'

We went downstairs. 'How is he?' I asked.

'As well as can be expected.'

'Is he going to . . . ' I faltered. 'Is he going to get any better?'

The doctor was exchanging looks with my mother. Death is a conspiracy, to be kept out of the way, but I was a child no more and could be told. 'No,' said the doctor, using his sick-bed voice. 'He isn't going to get any better.'

I had known already, but unspoken thoughts are different. 'I understand.' We saw the doctor to his Plymouth and watched him drive away. The weather was still poor; the night was dark. After I had shut the door I realised I was cold.

I returned to my father. He was quite still on the bed. I suddenly worried I might not be able to tell when he was dead, and the thought seemed irreverent and even dangerous. My mother joined me. We sat either side of the bed, as she and the doctor had done, and were silent a long time. My mind started to drift a little. Twenty-four hours back I had been in the Cotton Club. Now I am with my father who has had a stroke. Stroke is a peculiar word. I think of cats and children's hair. Is my father stroked? I wondered. No, he is stricken. Stricken; struck. The downward force of a hammer striking a heart, a heart that is also a clock. The delicate mechanism jars and jams. The clock strikes aimlessly, repeatedly. It will continue to strike that way until the mechanism runs down.

'How long?' I asked.

My mother misunderstood. 'He was fine Thursday afternoon,' she said. 'He played golf. Then he was dizzy and sat down. In the Club House. It happened in the Club

House. Jack Brecci brought him here.' I took her bulletins without complaint, but I realised I did not want to know. If he died soon I could go to China. I did not want to know that either, and could not forget it.

We stayed with him until ten, when a pretty Irish nurse came to relieve us. I wrote to Roscoe that night, care of his hotel in Hollywood, and told him it would be over soon. Then I tore up the letter and drafted another telling him to go without me. When I went to bed the second letter was in pieces too.

The following day I received a letter from him, posted in Washington, DC. The Secretary of State had called him back to the capital to go through his itinerary, though Roscoe suspected the idea was to try to get the expedition called off altogether. The situation in China was more stable than it had been for several years, and Secretary Kellogg did not want American interests jeopardised by American nationals doing damn fool stunts. And anyway, the Roosevelts were also setting off in an attempt to shoot this poor bear: one expedition might be adequate; two seemed downright wasteful.

'I'll get this sorted out pretty quick, but I shan't get to Hollywood until the end of the month,' Roscoe had written. 'I hope your father is·well.' The letter was signed for Mr Hamilton by a secretary. I did not care. What mattered was the delay.

My father's room was kept dark. What light there was seemed to collect round the chamberpot, the china washstand, and his face. For days there was no change. Then he seemed to recover a little. His speech returned and my mother was delighted at the ill-formed noises he made. The same noises scared me: he had once been a connoisseur, a taster of words, rolling them round his mouth before spitting them delicately into conversation; now he was a mute, cleft-palated, almost dumb, and mumbling through a barrier of misunderstanding like a comedian desperate for laughs.

'Torn,' he told me. 'Torn.' The sleet was heavier. The wind turned it against the window, turned it away again. In the gloom the washstand was an orchid that flowered at night. 'Torn.'

'He wants you to talk,' said my mother. 'He's saying you should talk to him.'

'Torn,' confirmed my father.

'What shall I say?' I asked my mother.

'Gegging,' said my father.

'Anything,' said my mother.

From where I sat I could see only the good side of his face. 'Eh!' he said, untranslatably insistent.

I told him what was interesting me most. I told him about China. I talked of the plans Roscoe had made: how we would leave San Francisco and travel to China via Hawaii and Japan. We would dock at Shanghai and travel up the Yangtze-kiang to Szechuan, and in the mountains of Szechuan we would hunt the pandas. I mentioned the film crew Roscoe hoped would accompany us, to take newsreel pictures of his success, and I talked about the Lolo bandits we might meet in the mountains. I described Szechuan as I understood it, with its terraced paddy-fields climbing up its hillsides and its system of irrigation based on ancient canals. Some canals are said to date back to Wen Wang, I told him, and then I thought I had better explain who Wen Wang was. He was the man who unified China, or the Middle Kingdom as the Chinese call it, three millennia or more ago. He had founded the first dynasty, the Chou. I told him how the martial Ch'in had succeeded the Chou, and of the Han dynasty, and of the building of the Great Wall, and of the number of people who had died in its construction. I described the fabled margin lands of legend, Yeuh and Takia-Makan, where demons and dragons lived; I talked a willow pattern on the washstand and filled the room with paper lanterns. I talked too much. He went to sleep, and when the nurse came I left him.

It snowed the next day, fat generous flakes that were black against the sky, white against the buildings and the trees. The snow made the room brighter, delivering daylight under the shutter like a note. In Monaco today the sun is shining; the temperature is almost in the seventies and I am almost in my sixties. My father's last illness happened a long time ago, so far back that he should be a stranger to me, but instead it is the voluble young man at the foot of the bed who seems the stranger; the old man I understand well. The old man watches his pacing son. The son wants to go to China. You lie there, troubled; you see him pace back and forth, and wonder what has gone wrong. For you there is no longer any China; for you there is only America.

You wanted America so much. Do you remember the San Francisco earthquake, and the rebuilding that began before the rubble cleared? It was a good time despite the deaths. It was a time when things were happening. The small bank you founded grew bigger, attracted offers from larger banks. You accepted one and moved East, director now of a national company, an American company, a pan-American company. You were rich, and now you had a son. You wanted America for your son.

Chinese was banned in the house. He was sent to the best private schools, this boy who talks now of China. You gave him Babe Ruth, the Tin Lizzie, the Chariot Race Sign. You gave him America. You watch him, exhausted. Your eye droops and then shuts. Death will be rather like this.

The young man's talk fills him now. He has been reading while you have been sleeping. He talks of the evil warlord Ts'ao Ts'ao, the theatre's legendary blackbrowed villain. He speaks of the founding of the Wei dynasty; they called this time the Three Kingdoms, because after

Ts'ao Ts'ao had proclaimed his own son first of the Wei lords, two rival dynasties appeared, the Shu Han of Szechuan and the Wu of Nanking. It was an era of heroes: I was just coming to speak of these when my father thrashed his head on the pillow and said, with a terrible, quiet lucidity, 'No!'

Do not speak of Chin, you are thinking. Do not speak of China. That is done with. Speak to me of America. Speak to me of my States.

I stood quite still looking at him. I thought he must die but he was strong. The working eye watched me though the other lolled and was lost. I drew my hand over my face and let it fall impotently to my side. 'I'm sorry,' I whispered, and then, 'Father.'

I called for the nurse and left him. I walked out of the room and out of the house. The snow was maybe seven inches deep by now: there had been a delivery of provisions that morning and where the truck had turned in front of the house was a circular track I followed. It led me round and round, round and round, which was where I wanted to go. I was too cold to smoke; I walked in circles and thought in circles, and my thoughts made me feel like Oedipus.

My body began to smart with the cold. I let it. It was bad enough to realise how dumb I had been, to talk of China to a man who had turned his back on all that. Worse, much worse, was the sense that I had known my talk of China would hurt him. I dared follow my thoughts no further.

At last I went in. My hands were white, the rims of my nails and the moons were blue. I forced myself to write to Roscoe, holding the pen between useless fingers and spoiling several attempts. I wrote what I should have said long before. I told him I was unable to leave my father; I told Roscoe not to wait.

He replied before three days were out:

Going nowhere without you.

There was an unexpected thaw and the poor white kids from Uptown waited in the gutters in case it washed luck their way. I remembered the hot black kids in Harlem waiting by the hydrants, hoping the same dream. Ours is a land of such extremes, but there are always those so poor they must wait in the gutter. In America everything is possible, my father had said, and I wondered if this were true.

He died at the end of October, during a few mild days in a bad winter. We had known it was near the day before. He had stopped breathing twice. I read him the sports reports and quoted the price of General Motors stock. He tried to smile in return; we understood each other now. The third time his breathing stopped the doctor could do nothing, did not try too hard. He closed my father's eyes and asked that we call the mortician.

I did not stay for whatever the mortician did, though my mother helped. I went for a walk, across the street and down to the lake edge. There was a jetty I knew jutted into the water of Michigan. It was a crude wooden construction of planks lashed to uneven posts, and I had often sat on one of those posts, third one along on the right-hand side, with a heavy coat and a carton of Lucky Strikes, watching the water grease and rainbow behind the boats. I did that then. The sun, which science tells us never moves, moved across the sky, and the lake went on for ever.

The world when my father died was sharply seen, grieving, grey and engraved, full of silly details that worried at the edge of my mourning. A spruce tomcat insinuated himself in the roots of a twisted tree and coiled himself into a threat. A gaggle of geese passed overhead. The water up close was murky, and the water in the distance was silver.

An hour passed and I returned to the house. My mother was alone at the foot of his bed. His eyes were mercifully shut, I thought, and then I wondered at the treachery in the thought.

My mother's eyes were also closed. She sat by the bedside still, like one who keeps a vigil. The mortician had gone and my father was dressed and ludicrously smart. I liked his face better now, doctored and waxy, and knew it better too. I smiled at the dead old man sadly, and wished him well.

'Edmund,' said my mother. 'What shall we do for his spirit?'

I looked across the body of my father at her. I did not understand.

'Where shall we build the shrine?'

We had a burial lot reserved in a cemetery west of the city. 'What do you mean?'

'For his spirit. So we can ask for advice and *feng shu*.'

My school was Episcopalian. The Jewish boys did not attend service, and we had no Catholics there, but the rest of us were herded into the hall where we heard the chaplain read from the English Bible and confuse God and the States. It was not much of a faith: like most people, I can only believe in God at God-forsaken times. It was not much of a faith but it was all I had. No one had told me about spirits.

My mother was weeping now. *Feng shu*, the Chinese word for luck, had released her tears. I looked at her in surprise. For thirty years she had been my father's wife, subservient, vaguely insubstantial. She had eaten American food and worn American clothes and contributed to the same charities as the neighbours. But mourning turned her, atavistically, to China.

Her tears were noisy, and I was jealous of them. She was accommodating her grief the traditional way, first indulging and then assuaging it by committing his spirit to guide and protect us. I had no such tradition, and the

85

Christian Heaven was too cold for comfort.

I walked around the bed. I knelt beside my mother. Her ancestors were my ancestors, after all. I knelt beside her and shared her tears. My father had joined our ancestors; he had become one of the drift of spirits collecting about the family. Where do these spirits live? I wondered. In China? And then I knew that they lived wherever we lived. I had never seen them before, but now the room was full of them. I held tight to my mother and, kneeling, we wept ourselves out.

There was an obituary in *The Tribune* and a wreath from the golf club. He would have appreciated both those tributes, as he would have appreciated the Stars and Stripes at permanent half-mast above the cemetery gates. The flag was gay, almost garish, against the clouds.

It was a quiet funeral on a cold day. The footprints left at the bottom of the grave by the workmen had frozen over, and when the casket was lowered the ice cracked and reared up, sharp and angular, like ruins in old excavations. The wind hurt my cheeks and made them blush; the flag rapped the flagstaff; the earth thumped and scattered on his casket. We left, and when I got home I called up everyone I still knew in Chicago. Some of them called me back and I went out that evening, to a downtown speakeasy. It was a restrained, noisy, happy evening, and when I got back to the house I packed.

My mother came with me to the airport. I should have felt guilty for leaving her so soon, but to feel guilty for travelling is not the American way. Instead, I kissed her briefly. There was snow piled up and soiled at the side of the runway; the black dress she wore was blacker against the heaps. I climbed aboard and waved to her. She did not see me, I think. Then the aeroplane was accelerating, taking off into the wind, and a flock of birds was startled into the air. When I next looked I could no longer see her, only the plane's shadow as it made a cross on the snow.

And so I journeyed West, for the first time in my life, as the prelude to my journey to the East. It was an unmemorable journey. We flew maybe a day, though the time difference confused me, and then circled above a city of lights, lost height, and landed. The last things I saw before the plane put down were the lights of Santa Monica on the rim of the world and beyond them, like a Pole Star, the single light of a ship on the sea.

The airplane taxied to a halt.

7
Hollywood

The night was warm, and so was the contrived smell of the night-blooming jasmine that blew in from the canyons. I walked across the apron to the control tower. Its lights were friendly and modern, and the girls who checked my ticket were all blondes.

A cab took me to my hotel. I checked in. 'Is Mr Hamilton staying here?' I asked.

'No sir,' said the man behind the desk. 'Yours is 345.'

'You're sure Mr Hamilton isn't staying? Mr Roscoe Hamilton, the big-game hunter?'

'Quite sure, sir. The elevator boy will help you find your room.'

'And there's no message?'

'No, sir.'

I took the proffered key and fetched out Roscoe's last letter. 'We're at the Hotel Hollywood this week. I've a room for you when you get in. Hope the funeral went well.' *This week* seemed the significant part, now I thought about it; still, Roscoe would be in touch.

I was hungry. The foyer had a sort of eleven-at-night emptiness about it, and the diner looked full. I went up to my room, washed and changed, and returned to the first floor.

The *maître* wore a blue sash beneath his monkey jacket and a medal ribbon in his lapel. He looked like a member of the Russian royal family. He probably was. 'Has Mr Hamilton of Westhouse been in at all?' I asked, leaving Roscoe's name like a tip.

The *maître* summoned a waiter who asked a bell-hop to

fetch a book. There was a consultation. 'Mr Hamilton will dine at midnight.'

'I see.' I decided on a gamble. 'Mr Hamilton is a very good friend of mine, and I'm sure he'll want to see me, but I'm also very hungry. Do you think you could let me have Mr Hamilton's table? He can join me when he arrives.' I had read my movie magazines; I knew as well as anyone that tables at the Hollywood were allocated strictly according to movieland power, radiating in rings of diminishing magnitude from the money-men who sat by the floor show to the fallen idols wedged against the walls. Roscoe, a millionaire gun manufacturer and socially desirable sharpshooter, would warrant a good table; an unknown Chinese like me would be lucky to get a seat at all.

'This way, sir,' said the *maître*, and I was so surprised I almost forgot to follow.

The *maître* handed me over to the junior waiter. The dining room was decorated with columns of light. Ritzy glittering pillars supported cascades of silver arches, and vast potted plants ran amok between the tables. A space was cleared for dancing, and the band blew out 'The Black Bottom', a little dated but still good for a good time. The bandleader's carnation was purple.

Around me were faces I knew from the movies. A full-lipped woman whose dress was stitched with pearls read the palm of a leading man. A fleshy dark Turk, his hands embellished with gold, pulled at a gross cigar. I smelt beefsteak and tobacco and perfume.

We passed the exclusive strip where the élite ate. Thin wreaths of smoke mingled in the expensive air. Then we were among the more tightly packed tables of the had-beens and would-bes, and the waiter led me to the very edge of the room.

'Are you sure this is Mr Hamilton's table?' I asked. 'Mr Hamilton of Westhouse?'

'Sure I'm sure,' replied the waiter. 'Sit down.'

I had to push my way through to get to the chair. This was not the table Roscoe Hamilton would have; maybe there was another Mr Hamilton of Westhouse dining there that night, a salesman or a junior executive? Next to me a fat man gnawed at a chicken bone. He chewed with relish, and greedy beads of sweat jostled on his temples.

The waiter had gone while I struggled to my seat. I waited for him to return. Nothing happened. The floor show was out of sight from where I sat; I could see a man in profile who might have been Lon Chaney, but who probably wasn't.

I tried attracting the waiters' attention. They ignored me. The man who might have been Lon Chaney lit a cigarette and I lit one too.

At last a waiter came, to collect my fat neighbour's plate. Whilst the fat man ordered pastries I slipped in a request for a bowl of chowder. Next to me a couple in hired evening clothes argued over the check. She swore to hit him when they got outside; he didn't seem prepared to wait till then.

My fat neighbour was served first. Hungry, I watched him eat. It was a calculated performance. His big hand closed voluptuously round a cream cake and brought it to his lips. I heard the smacking sound as he sucked the cream out and through his teeth, and saw him penetrate the shell of the pastry with his tongue. The tongue writhed and scooped after a cherry; he looped the fruit into his mouth and followed it with the rest of the cake, chewing now with his mouth open because he could not get it closed. When he chewed, the folds of fat at the back of his neck wobbled.

I turned away, to face the arguing couple. He told her they shouldn't have come. I wanted to be seen, she said. Fat chance in this place, the man replied. He waved the check. And the cost of hiring the tuxedo, he said. Hush, she said, I wanna go home. She began to cry. I turned back again.

90

The fat man had an éclair. He thrust the tip into his mouth and nibbled rapidly, ecstatically. His greasy chin quivered with pleasure and his eyes were quite closed.

At last my chowder came. Its fish smell was sharp and refreshing, a witty woman among these diners. I took a sip, and the fat man belched.

I was watching the door in case Roscoe did show. A man on his own handed his hat and scarf to the hat-check girl, who smiled beautifully and habitually and tidied them away.

I took another sip. The soup was tepid, and too salty.

A junior waiter was threading the new customer through the tables towards us. The newcomer was greyhaired and slight, and his face was almost familiar. The waiter motioned him to sit down opposite me.

'That's Mr Hamilton's seat,' I told him.

The waiter nodded. 'And *that's* Mr Hamilton.'

It was strange: the newcomer did resemble Roscoe; I knew the face had reminded me of someone. He had the same eyes and the same rather handsome full upper lip. Twenty years younger, this man might have passed for Roscoe's brother.

'You enjoying that?' asked the stranger abruptly, pointing at my chowder.

'Not much,' I admitted.

The pseudo-Hamilton waved the waiter away.

The flight must have taken longer than I had realised. About twenty years longer. This man even had Roscoe's voice. The thought occurred to me that perhaps this was Roscoe in disguise: after all, we were in Hollywood, the land of make-believe. If a make-up department could make a Madonna of Clara Bow it could surely make an old man of Roscoe; I felt the urge, fortunately resisted, to tug at one of the features extraneous to Roscoe, the veined red tip of the nose maybe, or the bulbous and slightly hairy lobes of the ears.

'You read the script?' demanded the stranger.

'Excuse me?'

'Have you read it?' He sounded vaguely belligerent. I have often suspected that the worst trait of my nature is that I take the line of least resistance: I simply shook my head.

'You should,' he said. 'It's got *words*.'

Words were beginning to matter in scripts. This was the Fall of 1927; *The Jazz Singer* had just been released, and had proved a sensation. I, who had watched Hollywood films in Paris and German films in New York, rather regretted the passing of the silent movie. No one else seemed to.

'You're not enjoying that at all, are you son?'

I pushed the chowder to one side. 'Cold.'

'Put some of this inside you to warm you up,' he said, producing a large silver flask from inside his pocket. 'I guess you'll want to see the set.'

'What set?' I asked, but he ignored me. He was concentrating on filling the two water glasses on the table without being spotted by a waiter.

'Bottoms up!' he instructed.

'Bottoms up.' I took a drink. The liquid was clear; it was probably paraffin. I gagged and put my glass down, barely tasted, while he refilled his own.

'Drink it down,' he commanded. 'A bit of moonshine never hurt a soul.'

It was not my soul I was worrying about. I shook my head.

'Drink it!'

He was not joking. I lifted the glass and swallowed rapidly to force the liquid past my tongue.

'Say,' said the stranger, perfectly amicable now. 'Why'n't we go look at the set tonight:'

'What time is it?'

'Twenty minutes gone twelve.'

The moonshine burnt holes in my resolve as well as my

stomach lining. Roscoe would not be coming now. 'Sure,'
I said. 'Why not.'

I pushed past the fat man and made for the exit. A
waiter appeared, wanting not unreasonably to know why I
was lcaving without paying. 'His soup was cold,' said my
companion.

'No,' I said. 'I don't mind paying. Put it on the
room-check: 345; name of Sin.'

'Sir?'

'Sin. S for Essence, I for Eyeball, N for Enemy. Got
that?'

'Sir.'

Frail though he appeared, my companion made better
time than I. We rendezvoused at the revolving door.
'Hate those things,' he said, and when I entered the door
he followed me into the same segment so that there was
no room for either of us to move. 'I told you I hated
them,' he said. 'We're stuck.'

'No we're not,' I said. 'All we got to do is push.' I leant
my weight on the door, shuffled my feet, and we were
undignified but free. 'Easy as that.'

Outside were the couple I had sat by. Honey, I love
you, you know that; sure honey, I love you too. I wanted
to retch, but that may have been the moonshine or the
revolving door.

'I guess you'll need a drink,' said my companion. 'Make
it quick. We haven't got all day.'

'Night,' I corrected, taking the flask. 'We haven't got
all night.'

'That's right!' he exclaimed, as though this were a new
notion. 'We haven't got all night.'

He did sound like Roscoe, damn him. I looked at him
again, trying to work out which features were Roscoe's
and which not, but I could not do it. Some people can
draw caricatures: they can capture a face with a couple of
exaggerated lines; I cannot do this. I saw a face that
reminded me of a face I knew, and heard a voice I thought

I had heard before, and was befuddled by this and by moonshine.

I handed the flask back. The fat diner was pushing through the swing doors now, his belly smudged by the glass. I suppose I was poisoned by this time. My thoughts were all oblique. The blondes at the airport were too lovely; the winter air too warm and fragrant; when the fat man clutched at his chest and collapsed, until his weight thrust the revolving door round and vomited his corpse into the street, it was just another unreality.

'Let's get out before the cops come,' said my companion, looking without interest at the body on the sidewalk.

The loving couple had moved on, and the hotel staff had not seen the man fall. 'Where are we going again?' I asked.

'Going noplace again. We haven't been anywhere yet.'

The fat man rested peacefully at the foot of the hotel steps. The pseudo-Hamilton led me to his car.

It was an old-fashioned limousine that smelt of tobacco and leather. He drove me along Hollywood Boulevard and turned south at Hollywood and Vine. Already these names were icons. 'You read *Last of the Mohicans*?' he asked.

'Sure. Why do you want to know?'

'It's crap.'

We turned again and he stopped the vehicle. 'I guess we're here,' he said.

We got out by a pair of wrought-iron gates. Beyond was what looked like a park. 'Everyone must've gone home,' he said. 'We'll have to use your key.'

'I haven't got a key.'

'Of course you have.' I shook my head and made it clear I hadn't. 'We'll go over the wall,' he decided. 'I'll give you a push.'

'Oh – no!'

The wall was some nine feet high and the far side

entirely dark. It was topped, Spanish style, with pantiles, and I fell before I could jump.

The water, when I hit it, was cold but not deep. I stood, cursing and spitting, then waded towards a broken blackness in the wall that indicated the gates. I tugged myself through the slabs of water: there is nothing more resistant than the black waters of night.

I only fell down twice though in the whole journey to the shore, and although I was bedraggled my night sight was improving. It showed me gravestones. Nothing but gravestones. What were they filming, I wondered? I leant my weight against one of the property department tombs out of curiosity, but it refused to give.

Like everyone else in America I had seen Griffith's *Intolerance*, so I knew what movie sets could be like: Griffith had constructed great pillars, twenty feet across, surmounted by elephants whose trumpeting trunks heralded the King of Babylon. Even so, the fire department had considered the set a hazard and had it pulled down; these tombstones were as durable as marble, as I knew because I kept tripping over them, and they stretched away further than my night sight could see. Distracted, I chose to walk amongst them a while, and I marvelled at the love of detail that had gone into this set.

I went back to the gates though, pretty soon, and called 'Mr Hamilton!' loudly. There was no reply. Wriggling my head through the wrought iron I could peer up and down the street. There was no limousine either. Somehow, I was not surprised.

There was lettering set in the ironwork. I tried to make it out: it was reversed of course, to be read from outside, but I wasn't *so* drunk; I knew that. 'Hollywood' was easy to recognise; it was reading 'Cemetery' that took me a while.

I retired to the portico of a mock-Classical mausoleum. My stomach was being dissolved by the contents of my

95

erstwhile companion's flask and my head was lousy with tangents, but I must have slept anyway, for I awoke to the sun seeping over the Hollywood Hills and to a pain in my head like I had an airship inflating in there. When I moved, the airship caught fire.

The gates were open now, and a man was sweeping leaves. I tried to avoid him, for I was not up to company, but he saw me and did not care that I was Chinese and in a sodden tuxedo. 'Howdie,' he called as I passed. I thought I knew him from some old movie; I thought I had seen him as the King of Babylon.

I went out on the street. My eyes were not working too well. I found a sign that said Santa Monica Boulevard on a post that was topped by a bell. I walked from the post and the bell, and felt awful and tried not to fall.

There were cowboys on the street practising rope tricks, and midget women who pouted. I saw lovely children in bows dragged by their dreadful mothers, and a German soldier in dress uniform, *circa* 1914, wolf-whistling a party of nuns. There was a policeman turning somersaults to please a performing dog, and a man doing Charlie Chaplin, and a filthy-wet-sick Chinaman in the remains of his evening suit who walked circles around the block. But he was just one freak among a lot of freaks, and eventually he found his hotel.

I was paid no more attention there than anywhere else on my journey, for which I was as grateful as I was likely to be for anything that morning.

'Mr Sin!' said the girl at the desk. 'Letter for you.'

I took the letter and the elevator. Neither meant too much, though the elevator worried my stomach when it lurched.

My room was bright and cheerful. I wasn't. I hung the 'Do Not Disturb' sign on the door knob and walked in. I must have still been drunk, I suppose. There was a shade over the window but the sun was low and sneaked into the room. I went over to draw the drapes, and looked out

96

over Hollywood. They were pulling the Sheriff of Nottingham's castle down and erecting a half-size Big Ben. The towers of Notre Dame were plasterboard, and their backs were scaffolding pipes. Beyond, Baghdad spread out like a magic carpet tacked in place by minarets. I shut it all out and went to sleep, but Hollywood had usurped my dreams: there was nothing left for fantasy, and I dreamt of haberdashers and soapdishes and of streetcars.

I had never suffered genuine alcohol poisoning before, so these sensations were new to me. There had been a revolution in my body overnight, and an anarchist regime now reigned. Someone had daubed slogans behind my eyes, and I saw the world through a whirl of graffiti; meanwhile the new government was executing the reactionaries in my head, and ricocheting bullets rattled in my throat. Worse still, the leading anarchist had planted a bomb in my lower bowel, round and hard and black, and I could feel the fuse burning down.

Fortunately, the Hotel Hollywood was in many ways old fashioned, and there was a chamberpot in the room. Unable to climb back in bed, I slept on the floor.

Some time passed. I pulled the blankets over me and continued to sleep. I slept for seven years. A curse fell on the kingdom and no one woke me with a kiss. My dreams, feverish and corrupt, stank of stomach gases, and waking, when it happened, happened quickly. I even managed to stand. There was daylight beyond the drapes. The California sun streamed by, fertile as if with fishes. I did not disturb the drapes: if the sun flooded in I would drown. Instead I used the halflight. I looked into the mirror. My eyes were red-rimmed and reduced; my chubby face was chubbier; my hair seemed thinner and more greasy. I was still somewhere in the obscene land of fairy tales, but had turned into a pig, not a frog.

Finally I made it. Finally I worked it out. The solution was

97

dentifrice. If I could just get my mouth feeling better, everything else would follow. Outside, though, it went dark, and I returned to my bed. I dreamt pointless fevered dreams.

The following morning I was hungry which was reasonable. I had eaten nothing for – by my rough calculation – forty-eight hours. My watch had stopped but it must have been early because the lights outside the hotel were still on. There was a bathroom down the hall. While in the bath I remembered the note I had been given on arrival back at the hotel. I got out the bath and towelled myself dry. When I got back to the room I opened the envelope. The message was from Roscoe, and characteristically terse:

Plaza Suite, Château Marmont. See you soon.

I dressed carefully and opened the window. The room needed airing. After breakfast and a couple of invaluable cups of coffee I went to the reception and asked about the Château Marmont. 'Sunset Boulevard,' said the blonde on the desk. 'You can't miss it.' She asked if I wanted a cab, but I preferred to walk. I needed reminders I was alive.

I have been frequently told 'You can't miss it' and gone ahead and discovered I could, but the Château Marmont really is unavoidable, standing at the point where Sunset Boulevard becomes Sunset Strip and towering high above its neighbours. It was new then, but its Norman exterior, forbidding to my mind, made it look antique. Inside was panelling and red carpets. I crossed the red carpet to the elevator and asked for Roscoe's floor; the elevator boy wore a pill-box hat and was all dimpled cheeks and cheeky dimples. 'You in the movies?' he asked, hopefully.

'I'm afraid not.'

He looked at me dismissively and the elevator came to a hesitant standstill, lining itself up imprecisely like a man trying to match wallpaper; even when it had finally satisfied itself it left me with a half-inch step down. The grill door concertinaed to let me through, and expanded again, and I made my way down quiet corridors to the Plaza Suite.

A manservant let me in. Roscoe, in slacks and an open-necked shirt, sat at a table and held effortless court over a group of movie men. I knew they were movie men because of their clothes: they wore high boots, khaki shirts, knee breeches; when they were filming the cameramen amongst them would wear their peak caps back-to-front, like Cockney dustmen.

'Edmund!' said Roscoe. 'How are you doing!'

'Fine,' I lied.

'You're sure you're all right?' He sounded concerned. 'The strain . . . '

He meant *the funeral*: I felt better already. 'A stomach bug. I'm over it.'

'Good.' He turned to the movie men. 'Folks: this is Edmund Sin, who'll be accompanying us on the expedition. Edmund, I won't introduce you to them all – to be honest I've forgotten half their names.' They laughed dutifully. 'But this is Frank Wetherby, who'll be directing the team.'

I shook hands with Frank Wetherby. He had a pointed, rodent face, as if the midwifery forceps had grabbed him by the nose when they pulled, and though he was two inches taller than Roscoe, he looked four inches shorter.

'Actually Edmund, you arrived just in time. Frank's billed some time at the United Artists' lot. Apparently he won't be able to take close-ups in Szechuan, or something, so we're going to take the close-ups here and edit them into the action. That right, Frank?'

'Sure. Usual procedure.'

I guess I looked bewildered, but then bewilderment was becoming an established part of my repertoire. Roscoe laughed and clasped a hand to my shoulder. 'I know. It sounded like cheating to me too. But that's the way things

99

are done. So come on: we're going to put you in the movies; we're going to make you a star.'

The rest of the day was a hectic high-speed chase round the studios. Make-up, stills, close-ups, long shots. Roscoe demonstrated the loading and firing of a gun for the camera. He demonstrated it again. And again. And again. Finally Frank Wetherby, who had become a Very Important Personage the moment we set foot on the lot, was satisfied. I was told to sit on a papier-mâché boulder, warming my hands on a fire. The fire was real and the boulder soon happily alight. We shifted the wire remains of the boulder and tried again.

'Cut!' It was strange to be bullied by Frank Wetherby; he has seemed so contemptible in Roscoe's plush suite.

'What's the matter?'

'Clothes!' There was no denying Wetherby's supremacy here though. 'He's meant to be a Chink! Why's he dressed like a college boy?'

'I am a college boy.'

They found me a splendid robe of yellow silk, printed with dark blue dragons. Their tails swirled all over the cloth. I was given a wide-brimmed coolie hat and made to stand with my hands clasped together. 'No!' cried Frank Wetherby. 'Look *serene*.'

'I'm getting hot.'

'For Christ's sakes. *Act*, can't you?'

We tried again. I looked serene. A woman fastened long moustaches to my upper lip with cow gum. I was given a pair of sandals from Wardrobe. I wore the Chinese outfit over my lightweight Brooks Brothers suit: there were so many layers to my identity now I could have been peeled like an onion.

Frank Wetherby looked at me through a small square of blue glass that replicated the effects of black-and-white film and decided he could shoot his scene. They rekindled the fire for me and I pretended my hands needed warming.

'Hamilton! Walk up behind him now. That's good. And point your gun. Now Chinaman, he's going to jab you in the back. You're going to look scared and move away from the fire. Got that?'

We did our best. Roscoe giggled in the first take; I moved too soon and spoilt the second; the third went in the can. The cameras wore their reels of film above their heads like Mickey Mouse ears, and the klieg lights could not compete with the California sun.

'Cut! *Roll*! Take six! *No, no, no*! You're a *hero*, Hamilton. Scare the Chink. *Scare him*! That's better. Now, we'll reverse it. Jack, Le Roy, get the covers over the stage and fast. I want a night shot, right? Time is money, time is money. The Chink's going to creep up on Hamilton and jump him. Get him a new robe; he can't crawl about in that. And get those lights working but low. Good. Props: any boulders left? I'll have the lot. *Lights*! *Action*!'

I crawled through lightweight paper rocks, property knife in my hand. Ahead of me Roscoe relaxed in the glow of the fire. We were getting better at this acting business. I even tried to be silent, forgetting there would be no soundtrack to pick up the noise. I got close, closer. '*Now*!'

I hurled myself at him. Roscoe was fitter than me, faster than me. In fact as well as filmland. We fought for the upraised knife: he hooked a leg round mine and brought me down; the knife spun from my hand. 'Great! *Great*!' encouraged Frank Wetherby. And then, furiously: '*Stop laughing*!' It was no good though. I was spread-eagled on the floor; Roscoe sat on my chest pinning my arms to the ground; and the two of us laughed like lunatics. It was the end of shooting for that day. Frank Wetherby tried to retake the final part of the scene, but every time we started to fight we started to laugh.

'*Amateurs*!' said Frank Wetherby in disgust.

We returned to the Marmont in a limousine. 'That was great,' said Roscoe.

'It was all right for you. You were the hero. I can just imagine the captions Wetherby will use for that little lot: "Sometimes The Natives Are Less Than Hospitable. Even So . . . American Pluck Wins Thru!" '

Roscoe stretched. 'You'll be all right.'

'I'll be a laughing stock.'

'You'll be a star.' He chuckled again. It had been a ridiculous, wonderful day. 'Maybe United Artists'll see the rushes and want to sign us on. Hamilton and Sin: high drama, low comedy?' He smiled at me boyishly. 'I'm glad you're coming to China.'

I was glad too. I watched the sun set on the boulevards and the freakshow folk on the sidewalk. Hollywood sloped away in shades of sepia and I caught the scent of fragrant jasmine.

The elevator boy thought Roscoe might be a producer and did a soft-shoe shuffle between floors. We tipped him extravagantly. We were all movie hopefuls now.

8
Beverly Hills

That evening we went to Beverly Hills, in the straight-
eight Packard drophead coupé Roscoe was driving that
week. He looked content with the world; his hair was
watered and his face was calm. 'I reckon I might set up a
movie company,' he told me. 'I never knew it could be so
much fun.'

Why not? Roscoe could do anything; he was the man
who had shares in the moon.

We left the city limits, on our way to a party held by one
of Roscoe's millionaire friends, Sammy Kierns. Roscoe
drove steadily, turning along Mountain Drive toward
Lorna Vista. The night was warm: our headlamps picked
out innumerable insects that competed for the brightness.
We turned through smooth gateposts of distinguished
stone, from which no gates yet hung, and up an unpaved
drive. There was an area of grassland illuminated by a
thousand flares; beyond that a bandstand and a fat
marquee that looked like the king of glow-worms; the
silhouette of the mansion glowered from the hill, craggy
and roofless.

We found a parking lot. The lot had been rutted by the
wheels of construction vehicles, and then flattened for
tonight by a roller; the tyre marks had become the pressed
and preserved fossils of extinct gigantic snakes. The sound
of music drifted across the lawn as we climbed from the
car, and with it came intimate talk, broadcast on the
breeze. 'So what happened to him?' asked the girl in the
mink of the man in the broad-brimmed hat.

'Ach. Who care? He lost, doll, and here is no time for

losers. It is winners that worry us, damn right.' His diamond tie pin gleamed in the torchlight.

We walked into the lights, into a magical, fragile world of dance music and tuxedos and women in silver lamé dresses who drifted back and forth before our eyes like the patterns in the air between the projector and the screen. I was entranced. Suave handsome men with trim moustaches were balanced elegantly in the light of the flares and talking of polo, while gorgeous blondes in silk that crackled between light and shade smoked cigarettes through tortoise-shell holders and sipped champagne between scarlet lips.

Roscoe was speaking with someone he knew. I stood at the margin of their conversation a while and let a servant hand me a glass of champagne. Columns of bubbles rose there and burst. Nearby, a man I might have recognised from the movies spoke with a pert and pretty woman. 'I don't agree,' he said. 'All that the movies do is show what's going on. They're a mirror to nature.'

'Sure. A mirror from an actress's dressing room, you'd say? Surrounded by bulbs and topped with a star? The trouble with mirrors, dear boy, is they have the property of reversing the truth.'

He laughed, and they moved across the lawn.

The orchestra finished its tune and there was polite applause. Then came the first crisp notes of *Rhapsody in Blue*, curling round the clarinet. The orchestra joined in, a brief crescendo hunted for a rhythm, and then the piano emerged from a brassy tattoo. Rapid notes and scales of blue rose and fell across the keyboard, and the swift erratic tune kept breaking through them like the memory of love. But just as I was picturing her face, the piano was crashing down through the tones, smashing through the New York air, breaking up on to East 68th and lying there abandoned, dead.

I took another sip of champagne. The night air was filled with the music of dance halls, a sleazy syncopated hoedown that toured America in an instant, before the clarinet wailed again and found us back in Manhattan. A sophisticated string-section took a horse and trap round Central Park, and the piano still mourned the girl we all loved.

I walked away from the lawn, towards the wood and the lake. The music followed me, notes rising like the bubbles in my champagne. The house on the hill was sinister and tragic, and emphatic against the skyline. I passed conversations about stock prices and canapés, and then I was in the open space between the party and the lake, where only the couples went. I reached the side of the water and stared at its flat and unbroken surface wishing I had a stone to skim. Then I set off left, towards a bridge that led to an island.

The bridge was Hollywood Oriental in style, with a canopied central section that looked a good place for a cigarette. An ovation of fireworks exploded unexpectedly over the lake and into the lake; the sparks fell, met and extinguished their reflections. I heard voices from the island, whispers in the shrub. Clearly, I heard a man's voice saying, 'It was only the fireworks,' and then there was a quiet pause as if he was testing his statement. Then giggles, urgent ones, and his voice again: 'Come on peach, oh peach, oh come on.' I wondered how to leave without making any noise, and decided to finish my cigarette first. When I dropped it in the water, it hissed.

I did not know then how important this couple would be to me, nor how much confusion they would cause me: the man was Michael Hall, the English actor; the woman was Roscoe's wife. But then, at that time I did not even know Roscoe had a wife.

Another burst of fireworks splashed the sky and behind my eyes, so that for a moment or two the world was firework. I tiptoed carefully, sightlessly, off the bridge, and almost walked into a man who stood on the shore-path. It was the pseudo-Roscoe, and somehow I wasn't surprised that he was there.

'Hi!' he said. 'Didn't know you knew Kierns.'

'Oh. Hi.' There was no enthusiasm in my voice. 'Look, I must be moving. Nice to see you.'

'No hurry fella. I won't tell.'

Tell what? 'Oh?'

'I've gatecrashed a few parties in my time. Gatecrashed them with Sammy Kierns too.' A memory made him laugh and he looked out across the lake, where delicate reflections half hid and half revealed his face. He looked more than ever like an ageing Roscoe. It was the expression as much as anything, I guess, the wistful expression that recalls a lost dream. Then he turned to me and grabbed me hard by the elbow. I was annoyed until I realised he needed the support. 'Things I could tell you about Sammy Kierns!' he continued, his tongue ignoring his buckling knees. 'Did I tell you about the bathhouse?'

He steadied himself irritably, as if balance was a habit he was trying to break, but he still held my arm. 'No,' I said, resignedly.

'Every Sunday afternoon, straight out of church, Warren'd take me and a few friends. Nan used to go along too sometimes; I guess Warren was happier with her there really, made him feel more comfortable. And there was Sam I guess, and Al Fall if he could make it, and me week after week because I kind of liked the place.' I let him talk, while midnight chased an owl out of the trees and the sandalwood flavour of the Hollywood night closed in on this Beverly Hills Ruritania. 'The things we used to do. There was this dame knew a trick, could pick things up in her. You know, pick up coins and keys and that. I used to take Warren to watch her while Sam and Al talked money. Warren didn't like to know about these things; it was when he found out what was going on that we had to have him finished. I was sad about that; he was a nice guy.' I was not really listening, so I did not know exactly when I realised who he was talking about.

'You mean Warren Harding? The President?'

'Sure. Who'd you think I meant? Warren Peace?' The pun came so easily that I was sure he had used if before, but I was not interested in that. I suddenly knew who I was talking to, and was fascinated by the horror I felt.

'You're Calvin Hamilton.'

'Sure.' He started another 'Who'd you think . . . ' but remembered he had used the line. 'Who are you?'

'Edmund Sin.'

'Then you're not the guy from Universal? Guy I met a couple of nights back at the Hotel Hollywood?'

I shrugged politely. I felt no compulsion to help him out.

'You sure you're not the guy? You look a lot like him.'

'I'm Chinese,' I pointed out. 'We all look the same.'

'Hey. Maybe I blacked. I don't often black. Maybe I blacked that night.'

'Sure. Look, I must be going.'

'Blacked once in Connecticut. Lasted five months. Terrible thing that.' But I had left him before he could tell me any more. I needed to speak to Roscoe, to tell him his father was down by the lake shooting his mouth off. I heard neither the splash as the old man fell in, nor the noises he must have made as he drowned.

The party seemed to have grown tired now. The music haunted; a fat saxophone dominated, rounding up the clarinet and leading it back to the chain-gang. I looked for Roscoe: all around were men in tuxedos with watered hair, but he was not amongst them. The silk lapels of the tuxedos were the shape and texture of cobras' hoods, and inhaled cigarettes in ivory holders flashed bright and then disappeared like snakes' tongues.

Around the edge of the lawn couples walked, shadowed by husbands and the jealous wood. In the marquee coloured servants mixed the guests' drinks; the guests had mixed their drinks as well.

Eventually I found Roscoe, sipping champagne with a fashionable young lady with a pout. She spoke; he listened. I do not think he was disappointed when I interrupted them. 'Edmund,' said Roscoe. 'This is Paula Jaycee, a friend of my wife's, she tells me; Paula, this is Edmund Sin.'

I smiled at her and she smiled back. 'Can I speak to you?' I asked Roscoe.

'Sure.'

I drew him a little away from Paula Jaycee, and her Clara Bow pout tightened disagreeably. 'I think you ought to go speak to your dad,' I said.

'Is *he* here?'

'He's down by the lake. I think he's talking too much. About Harding and –'

'I guess I'd better take a look. Has he been drinking?'

'I think so.'

'There's a surprise.' He looked at Paula Jaycee – 'I'll not be long' – and left us.

'Have you known Mr Hamilton long?' I asked.

'I call him Roscoe,' she replied.

A waiter came by with an empty salver. I stopped him and asked for champagne. 'For two?' he asked. Paula Jaycee nodded.

'It's a good party,' I said.

'It's okay.'

A laughing couple joined us on the lawn and exchanged greetings with Paula Jaycee, who in her turn tried to introduce me. 'This is Edward . . . He's someone Roscoe knows.'

'Edmund Sin,' I supplied.

'Pleased to meet you,' said the woman, a rather handsome lady with a thin nose and good eyes. 'I'm Katherine Hamilton, Roscoe's wife, and this is Michael Hall, my dearest friend.'

'Roscoe said he'll be back in a moment,' said Paula Jaycee.

'He's gone to talk to his father,' I added.

'That drunk!' said Katherine Hamilton. 'Is he here? It's quite a family party. I wonder if Roscoe knows I'm here.'

'He didn't mention you,' I said.

'He doesn't.'

'Are you an actor, Mr Sin?' Michael Hall asked.

'No. I'm' – I wasn't sure – 'I'm going with Roscoe to China.'

'China now!' said Roscoe's wife. 'My. What a varied life the man leads!'

Paula Jaycee looked pleased when Roscoe returned; Katherine Hamilton looked completely indifferent. 'Hello, dearest,' she said. 'And how's daddy?'

'Edmund said where I'd gone, did he? I'm afraid I couldn't find my father.'

'That must have been a disappointment for you. Why's he in Hollywood anyway? Why are you?'

Roscoe was polite, and tried to be as disinterested as his wife. But I felt, for the first time since I had met him, that here he was at a disadvantage. 'Edmund and I are passing through on our way to Asia. Dad reckons to be making films, I heard.'

'So's Michael,' said Katherine Hamilton. 'But he's not very good at it either, are you pet?'

'Come on, Katherine,' said Hall. 'We really ought to be on our way.'

'Ah well. Drag me away from my husband if you must: after all, you always have.'

'Goodnight, Katherine,' said Roscoe.

'Night-night darling. So nice to have met you. Nice to have met you all.' They left, crossing the lawn busily.

'We ought to get off too, Edmund,' said Roscoe.

'You're going?' asked Paula Jaycee. 'We haven't had that little talk!'

Roscoe turned on her. 'I'm sorry. Edmund and I must leave. I'll be in touch when I get back to the States. Bye.'

She was probably the sort of girl who could summon

tears at will, so I did not feel sorry for her at all.

We walked back to the parking lot rapidly, with Roscoe setting the pace; he drove off just as rapidly, and silently. We raced through the wooded slopes. The moon came out and the world changed. We braked at a sudden bend and the car moved sideways towards the edge of the roadway, and then we were going just as quickly along the straight that followed. We were going far too fast.

I saw tail lights. I did not look as we passed a limousine that was returning from the party; I did not dare. Then there was another limousine, and a bend approaching, and I knew we were going to crash. The trees went by with brusque, colourless leaves; the thoughts that went through my head made me a movie. I thought of the comic cop car that stopped on the tracks, and the frantic idiot policemen pushing, pushing, as the up-train bore down. I imagined the disintegration as the chariot veered from the track, and the slow dust turning and churning; a wooden wheel was thrown into the air, and the gladiator sun spun on the wheel's wide scythe. I followed every frame as the man stood high on the upper wing of the plane, and the plane ploughed into the barn.

This time I could not even close my eyes, but stared at the bend ahead. The two cars 'were level as we started to turn, but the other did not want to compete and braked hard. Roscoe spun the wheel and we were through, safe the other side; as we passed I saw the white faces of Hall and Katherine Hamilton staring out. Roscoe drew his car up too.

I had looked at him while he was driving but had not seen him. Now, in this lull, I did see him; I saw him fully. I thought he would be scared, or exultant, or both. He was neither. He was calm, and quietly content.

Hall drove slowly round the bend. Katherine Hamilton lowered a window and called to Roscoe, 'Did you enjoy that, darling?' Hall sat behind the wheel of his Hispano

Suiza and looked blankly along the beam of his head-lamps.

Roscoe walked into the beams. 'I won,' he said, to Hall.

Hall made no reply. 'Play somewhere else,' suggested Katherine Hamilton.

Roscoe stood his ground. 'Just remember I won,' he said. He turned and walked back to his Packard, and the Hispano Suiza edged past. 'Drive carefully,' called Katherine Hamilton.

Our engine fired. Roscoe worked the shift. For the first time for what seemed a long time, he spoke to me. 'I should have kept away from her,' he said; 'I could have kept away from her,' he lied.

'Oh.' I was an innocent: my seed had been spent on a Parisian whore who would barely remember *le Chinois* she had served. Now I am a widower, another man who has been through a marriage: it sounds selfish, sounds stupid, but I believe that despite the pain of her cancer, my wife and I did better than Roscoe.

Roscoe was still scratching at a wound that he wouldn't let heal. 'I won,' he said. His voice was as emotional as that of a man ordering his secretary to order flowers for his wife, and his indifference was only his habit. 'I'm glad,' he continued. 'But she isn't worth it, Edmund. No woman is.'

I was glad he felt that way. He may have won the race, but I knew he had lost the prize.

'I'm tired of Hollywood,' he said. 'Let's go north tomorrow. Let's just get out of here as soon as we can.'

Behind us, in the hills, Sam Kierns' half-finished house was blazed with light, and Calvin Hamilton was dead beneath the waters of the lake.

'I loved that woman,' said Roscoe, and his words made me sad.

Late October evening. My memory is fine. I was glad to

be done with the States then and I am glad to be done with them now. It will be good to write at last about China.

But first I must get to China: we sailed on my birthday, and the liner was called *The Pearl*; the California we left behind was wrapped in fog, and because the rest of the world was hidden, things visible grew in significance and substance. I watched the water-drops hanging from the ropes tied round the lifeboats' hulls. The vibration of our engines shuffled the drops into one another, but marriage made them too heavy and they dropped: I felt miserable as hell and did not know why.

Roscoe joined me on the deck. 'Lousy day,' he commented. San Francisco had already disappeared; our voyage was accompanied by a clear globe half full of water and bordered by mist. An island floated into view, forbidding as a mine. I guess it might have been Angel Island or even the Golden Gate headland, but to me, on that water and on that day, it looked like Alcatraz.

'You don't look happy we're under way,' said Roscoe.

'It must be the fog. It makes me sad.'

'It hides America,' said Roscoe, and I realised that for him this was a blessing. It was not only the fog that made me sad, however: I was constantly finding new things to worry me; that week I was obsessed by a fear of chopsticks.

We went into the saloon. Roscoe never drank much, maybe a single cocktail a day, and I usually followed his example when in his company. That day, however, I just kept pouring it down: it wasn't to celebrate my birthday; it was to help fend the questions Roscoe asked about China.

'I don't understand the political thing at all. Can you explain the situation for me so I can get it clear in my head?'

'It is complicated,' I said, wondering if I understood

any more than he did. But I have two talents. One is the good fortune to be places where things happen; the other is the ability to simplify facts: I was a good newsman in my day. I had read a lot about China, and had practised what I wanted to say on my father who did not want to know. Now was the time to make use of that knowledge.

'Chinese history,' I told him, 'only really becomes complicated this century. For the previous three thousand years it had been pretty straightforward: the dynasties changed but the system didn't; the emperor ruled and the people worked.

'Holding this together all those years was Confucian philosophy. Nobody really knows for sure who Confucius was or even whether he really existed; not all that many people even knew much about his teachings. Like Christianity in Europe, and I guess in the States too, it was accepted: things were organised this way because that was the way things were organised. The success of Confucianism is that it reflects the conservatism of the Chinese.' I suddenly wondered if I should use 'us' or 'they' to speak of the Chinese. 'There are too many of us for change to be popular, or even all that possible; too many people trying to co-exist will tend to prefer things as they are, however lousy, rather than risk making some huge irrevocable mistake.' But, despite the innate conservatism of which I had spoken, I had made the radical choice; I had chosen to speak of *us*. I continued. 'Change, when it came, came from outside, from Europe. The Westerners brought trade, gunboats, syphilis and the Bible. Their un-Oriental energy drove Chinese businessmen from the ports and Chinese soldiers from the barricades. China, the Middle Kingdom, the centre of the universe, became virtually a colony, like America was in the eighteenth century, except that in China the Indians were actually probably more sophisticated than the invaders.'

'You know, I've always seen you as an Indian,' said Roscoe. 'As an Uncas or a Chingachgook.'

I ignored the interruption. 'The parallel isn't exact. There are a lot more Chinese than there ever were Indians – a lot more Chinese than there ever was anyone, for that matter – and we're also good learners. A lot of Chinese saw what was happening to their country and wanted to learn how it was that a few white-skinned foreigners could make the Emperor look like a cypher; once they started to look, they found a thousand things that were wrong. The whole concept of the Empire was obsolete, they saw, and everything was run in an archaic, anachronistic way that made it easy for the Europeans to infiltrate and take charge. Some who saw this responded with revolution; some sent their children to Europe or the States to be educated. Many, like my parents by the way, just got out and left backward, depressed China to get on with its decline, while they sought greater opportunities abroad.

'Anyway, by 1912 there were a lot of people in China who were ready to overthrow the Emperor and bring in a more up-to-date, twentieth-century method of ruling. It's kind of odd: the most patriotic, nationalistic Chinese in those days were also the most Westernised. They took the American Revolution as their model: the foreigners would be thrown out, and there would be a new republic established in the land.

'But after Confucius, confusion. China was meant to be a democracy, but the people who held the elections also held the guns, and these people, the Warlords, the provincial military governors, became the effective rulers. Their rule lasted from 1912 right up to the beginning of this year.

'The empire, by the way, was fragmented, but the idea of it wasn't forgotten, least of all by the Warlords. Most of the Warlords had designs on the Heavenly Mandate . . . '

'The what?'

'The Heavenly Mandate. The throne of China'

'I see.'

114

' . . . but the only way any Warlord could achieve his ambition was to ally himself with some other Warlord, because the Warlords knew full well they couldn't rely on the people for their support. They'd been too harsh. And of course, if the only way of augmenting their power was by alliances that also diluted it, no one Warlord was able to get strong enough to rule. Autocracy can't be shared.

'The trickiest part to describe is the most recent. All I can tell you about is what I've read in the newspaper reports. But as long as you don't mind that, I'll do my best.' Roscoe signalled another drink for me; the assiduous waiter brought it at once. 'China has changed a lot since the days of the empire, but often in ways that weren't that obvious until this year. For one thing, the Westerners had taught us new business techniques, and there's a whole new class of workers, factory workers, in China today.'

'Communists?'

'Not necessarily. Just men who worked together in factories and had the chance to meet together and talk things through. They were democrats, I'd say, like the Americans: they believed in Dr Sun Yat-Sen's vision for the future, which would make China the sort of country where everyone would be equal before the law, with an equal vote and equal opportunity.' I was aware, even through the martinis, that this was an idealised view of America, and an even more glamorised view of any possible China. Still: 'Dr Sun Yat-Sen led a political party, the Kuomintang, the ones in charge now. The Kuomintang are the Nationalists, and they'd been successful in the elections but hadn't been powerful enough to take away the power of the Warlords.

'Sun died a couple of years back, and his successor, Chiang Kai-shek, is a much more aggressive man: last year he led the Nationalists on a march from Canton to the Yangtze in what's become known as the Northern Expedition. It was almost a second revolution; the Warlords were vanquished and Chiang is now leader of the whole country.'

I was proud of using the word *vanquished*; I stopped talking and savoured the sound for a moment, and Roscoe asked me about the Bolsheviks. It was the sort of question a multi-millionaire might be expected to ask, I guess.

'They've no influence,' I reported confidently. 'They used to be part of the Kuomintang but they were all kicked out.'

We talked a while longer and then went to bed. I felt triumphant: I had survived the interrogation I had feared. But actually, three fallacies had already crept into my narrative.

First: the reputation of the Kuomintang in 1927, while *The Pearl* sailed for China and I sank too many martinis, was very high. They were known to be fair-minded and honest. I believed in them. But subsequent stories have thrown doubt on this reputation: after all, the Communists weren't 'kicked out' of the Kuomintang, they were betrayed and then butchered.

It happened like this. Sun Yat-sen admired the Communists and their organisation, and in 1922 he invited them to join the Kuomintang. Because they were well organised, they soon became very influential, especially amongst the factory workers on the coast. At the beginning of 1927 they organised a strike in Shanghai which was designed to cripple foreign businesses.

The Western powers united against the strikers, of course. The British alone sent forty thousand troops to Shanghai; soon the strike was beleaguered and its leaders were crying for help to Chiang and the Nationalist forces. Chiang sent in his troops: they pretended to join with the strikers and then murdered them all to a man. In 1927 it never occurred to me that the Kuomintang could commit atrocities; in 1927 that is probably what the Jews were thinking about their beer-and-Beethoven loving neigh-bours.

Secondly, I said that the Communists no longer had any influence. The evidence certainly pointed that way: we did not know how it had been done, but we knew that they had been removed from the Nationalist government; we knew some survived in the hills of Kiangsi, south of the Yangtze, but we thought of them as bandits soon to be wiped out.

And thirdly, here in 1963, I apparently cannot trust even my memory. For I know I could not have spoken so well, nor for so long. Not even on my birthday.

But history is not what happened in the past, it is what we are told happened in the past. The pen probably is mightier than the sword – I have no sword, but I can recount this history and hope it will be believed – yet all too often the pen has been in the hands of the man with the sword. Even now, forty years on, we cannot really say what happened in China. We had the Kuomintang history of events, followed by the Communist history of events. Same events, different history. If you read between the lines of any story, including mine, you find the blank spaces where the truth is to be found.

CATHAY

9
The Pacific

The news of Calvin Hamilton's death reached us two days out. The Captain drew Roscoe aside and broke it to him in person, but as the telegraph operator had already told the Chief Steward, and the Chief Steward had informed his staff, the Captain could just as well have made the announcement on the Tannoy for all the secrecy there was aboard ship.

Had the news simply said that Calvin Hamilton was dead, there would have been no rumours. As it was, we learnt that he had been found drowned in the lake of Sammy Kierns's half-finished mansion, and that a witness had placed Roscoe Hamilton in the vicinity just after Calvin had last been seen alive.

By mid-morning, the rumour that Roscoe had been involved in his father's death was as good as confirmed. I was sitting in my cabin, wondering what I should have been thinking, about Calvin and about Roscoe, when the sound of a shot broke through the familiar vibrations of the ship's turbines.

At the second shot I went on deck; by the third I was crowding like everyone else aboard, towards the stern of the ship. There Roscoe stood, dressed in a white polo shirt and yacht-club cravat, shooting seabirds out of the sky.

I was a level above him, and I looked down on him and the sun-blistered planks that were marked for deck quoits: the crowd refused to go nearer to him than the white painted lines permitted. He raised the barrel of the gun and fired again, turning a gull into a squall of feathers that idled on the wind.

A woman near me fainted. He fired another shot and another bird disintegrated. I felt like fainting too. I had a lot of fellow-feeling for the confused and wheeling birds: like them I felt I should do something, and did not know what to do. They continued to circle the stern, out of habit or because they had nowhere else to go, and Roscoe fired his gun and killed an albatross.

He was reloading when the Leading Seaman pushed through the crowd. The Leading Seaman wore muscular tattoos on his forearms, and had brought two sailors with him in case it came to a fight. It did not come to a fight. Roscoe listened politely to the Leading Seaman, and whatever was said must have sounded reasonable, for he handed his gun over and let the sailors escort him away.

The crowd kept off the quoits court. The sun continued to shine. In moments the birds' bodies were mangled and lost in our wake. I found myself part of a strangely subdued mob, their indignation less important than their sense of wonder. Roscoe had shot the albatross, and we were witnesses, wedding-guests, voyeurs.

I went to my bar, and then to my room. I wanted time on my own.

When we think of the moon we think perhaps of a crescent, or a semi-circle, or a sphere. We forget that, whatever the shape of the moon, it is only the shape the sun's light gives to it; and were it not for the sun, we should see no moon. Now it was as if the sun was locked in a cabin and I was in darkness. I felt I had never known such dark.

I was so certain, you see. So certain that Roscoe had murdered his father. I had the evidence all pieced together. One: I had met Calvin Hamilton by the lake; Calvin had been talking too much about things which reflected badly on the Hamilton family, the past presidency, and our host at the party. For all I knew, the implications of Calvin's story went further than that. Two: I had sent Roscoe to look for Calvin, and Roscoe had gone and returned, as other people had apparently witnessed too. Three: Roscoe had been in a strange mood and had driven away from the scene of the crime like a maniac. Four: he had hurried to leave the States. Five: he had shot those birds from the stern of the ship, and somehow, for everyone aboard, that seemed to be virtually a confession.

I do not think I am particularly selfish. It was only after I had thought this much about Roscoe that I began to be interested in my own situation, and realised I was in a heap of trouble.

Our next port of call was Hawaii, which was not a state in those days but was full of Americans nonetheless. It seemed inevitable that Roscoe should be returned to California for questioning, if not for trial, and I wondered what would happen to me then. After all, my status was unclear. I was Roscoe's unpaid companion, but he had paid for my berth. If he were taken off the ship, would I be allowed to remain on board? Would I want to? Or would I be asked to go with him back to the States, or forced to go with him, or refused permission to go back with him?

What did I want to happen?

I did not know. For a long time I had excused myself that, in deceiving him, I had not deceived an ordinary man; deceiving him was an achievement, not a sin. Suddenly he was no longer greater than ordinary men; he was worse in my eyes, and I had lost my excuse.

I knew I should feel disgust for him, and contempt.

I knew that I felt neither. He was Roscoe.

I was too young, too foolish, and out of my depth when I took my resolution. But I took it and believed in it and upheld it. I thought that I knew he was guilty, but I was determined to stand by him.

123

There are some five and a half thousand nautical miles between San Francisco and Shanghai if one travels direct; even allowing for the curvature of the earth, the detour to Hawaii must add at least another thousand. All Pacific liners stop there, however, because tourists just love Hawaii, the nubile land, home of steel-stringed guitars, garlanded maidens, smiling princesses and refrigerated beer.

We put into Honolulu four days after the bird-shoot. I had not seen Roscoe since then as he had been in confinement, nor had I mixed with my fellow passengers. The sight of land took me on deck, however. The atoll was refreshing and verdant; a tropical breeze wafted the trees; I heard the lilt of those distant guitars; and so on. I was more aware of a posse of Navy ratings and reporters who waited on the quay.

The gangplank was lowered and I watched as Roscoe was led off, accompanied by two seamen from the ship. He did not look worried, but I was seeing him from a distance. The deck was crowded and I stood in a crush of passengers who were curious to see the fate of the dreadful Mr Hamilton but who also wanted a chance to get at Paradise. We looked down on figures as foreshortened as their shadows. The reporters pushed forward and the sailors pushed them back. Flashlights flickered ineffectually in the sunlight. Meanwhile, Roscoe was having a short and apparently friendly conversation with a young officer, and then a sailor was sent aboard the ship.

I was still undecided about what I should do when I heard my name over the Tannoy: 'Would Mr Edmund Sin, go at once to the dock where transport will be provided.' I had to push through the passengers to get off, and by the time I was down the gangplank Roscoe had been driven away. I was shown to a second vehicle, and saluted. I had never been arrested, and did not know how it would feel, but I had not expected it to feel like this.

I was driven to an airstrip not far from the port, and there I rejoined Roscoe. There was no time for questions though. There was no time to question him, except with a look, and questions asked that way give no answers. Instead we were ushered on to an amphibious airplane, painted in the bright interwar colours of the Army Air Force, while the Navy man gushed his farewells. 'I'm sure you'll be very comfortable, sir . . . We're honoured . . . The Admiral asks after Mrs Hamilton . . . I hope you have a pleasant stay.' The amphibian was taxiing in a welter of sound, and taking off to a crescendo. We tilted our wings over the island and set off north. Conversation was impossible.

We landed just outside Pearl City, which is the far side of the bay from Pearl Harbor. In those days Pearl Harbor was not even a name to me, and though the blockhouse gardens and glasshouse blocks of its plan established it as a garrison town, the Navy had not yet turned it into US Fleet headquarters and the servicemen we saw were as often soldiers as sailors.

Again we were put into separate automobiles, and driven round the bay to a large white building, an official residence. Roscoe's car got there before mine, and by the time I arrived Roscoe was already shaking hands with a handsome white-haired man who wore a handsome white-and-gold uniform.

'Katherine tells me she's decided not to press the divorce,' the white-haired man was saying.

'I'm glad. I thought she'd give in. She never had any grounds.'

'Of course not.' The man shrugged. 'I sometimes think my daughter's a fool. I certainly don't understand why she can't just settle down with you and have children.' I felt uncomfortable and ignored as I listened to the conversation. The white-haired man was presumably Roscoe's father-in-law. I was beginning to think I knew more members of Roscoe's family than my own.

Roscoe was making excuses. 'We never really found time, I guess.'

'No. Well, come in anyway, make yourself comfortable. Maybe you and Katherine'll be able to start again now.'

'Maybe,' said Roscoe.

'Skipper of *The Pearl* reckons he had to arrest you? Thought you'd had something to do with your father's death?'

'Yes, sir.'

'Goddamned fool, your father. Always was. Still, I guess that's all done with.'

They started to walk towards the house. I found myself standing there like a waiter, and like a waiter I coughed. Discreetly.

'Hello Edmund,' said Roscoe, apparently noticing me for the first time. He introduced me to his father-in-law, Admiral Kerple.

'I hope you don't mind me asking,' I said, 'but did I hear you say Roscoe was no longer suspected.'

'Sure,' said the Admiral. 'Storm in a teacup. There was a couple on the island who actually heard old Calvin fall in, but they couldn't do a thing about it because they were balling.' He laughed loudly. 'Hell! You should've seen what the official communiqué said. "Disporting themselves amorously." I needed a translation! But tell me, Roscoe, what're your plans?'

'I'm carrying on with the hunt. I guess I couldn't get back to the States in time for the funeral anyway.'

'So you'll go back to *The Pearl*?'

'I guess, or we could stay on here in the islands until *The Resounder* gets here next week. I've arranged for a film crew to come to China with us, and they're sailing on *The Resounder* anyway.' He rubbed his face with his hands. 'I wasn't any too popular aboard *The Pearl*,' he admitted.

'Sure. Wait. Stay here. I'll send down to 'Lu for the

valises. After all, sounds like you're staying in the family. By the way, who was that good-looking English actor I met at your place once?'

'Michael Hall?'

'That's the one. He was the guy who was balling on the island.'

Roscoe pulled his lower lip back with his breath. 'Do you know who the woman was?'

'I can't recall. Name like J.C.'

Roscoe looked surprised, and then laughed. 'My God. They've said this in public, you say?'

'Sure. At the enquiry. I guess it'll be in the newspapers by today.'

Roscoe was still laughing. 'Somebody's been pretty smart,' he said.

I did not laugh with him. I knew how impossible it was for Michael Hall and Paula Jaycee to have been together on the island, and therefore I knew they could not have witnessed Calvin Hamilton's death. His alibi was a lie.

We stayed five days on Oahu. As I have never been much interested in things military I do not recall much of our time there: I remember a spitting, polishing sun that bounced off every surface, and a daily parade of soldiers performing their quaint gun-slapping drill in the park, and one day a battleship with its escort in the bay off Ford Island.

The battleship was sleek and low and dangerous. It had dead eyes where the anchors were stored, and a bloody mouth where the red rust-proofing paint curved up beneath the raked bow. The guns were dangerous too: designed to absorb the recoil, their barrels were like reversed telescopes, which was appropriate enough; a telescope brings things nearer, while a gun blasts them irredeemably away. There were little cutters and lighters servicing the battleship, and I thought of pilot fish.

On the Friday we said goodbye to Admiral Kerple and

were flown back to Honolulu to join our new ship. The camera crew was there of course, and Frank Wetherby was a bore, drinking too much and playing poker too well. But I was glad of their company nonetheless; I thought I needed to get away from Roscoe.

I was a fool, of course.

Our journey continued westward through the tropics. I had my porthole open almost all the time. We passed the Midways and then saw no land until Japan, where we sailed round the south island, which is called Kyushi, and into the port of Nagasaki. There were Japanese warships there, much like America's except for the lettering on their bows and the flags at their sterns; they were even powered by the same fuel, for the product of the Teapot Dome fraud had been sold to the Japanese Navy . . .

I had an American steward who helped himself to my cigarettes when I slept. 'See that building?' he invited, pointing through the porthole. 'That's the Jewelled Egg. Biggest brothel in Japan, I reckon. Don't dangle your bait there; you'll catch more'n fish.'

I thanked him for his advice. Curiously enough, in a town twinned by fate with Nagasaki, the woman who was to be my wife was born that month.

We crossed the East China Sea. Until then we had been lucky with our weather: the typhoon season was over and I had almost forgotten the sea could raise a storm, or that I could throw up my lunch. Both happened in quick succession: a rogue wind was reported off Hong Kong, and we watched indigo clouds on the horizon, shovelled up like earthworks and then turning the colour of earth as they shut out the sun. There was a pressure in our ears, like modern flying. And then there was storm, pure storm, dominating the elements and the senses. I was certain I would die.

The next day was calm, though overcast. The storm had

blown us north, though not far off-course, and we were close to the coast of China now. China's climate is not unlike that of the States: Shanghai is like South Carolina, Peking is like Nebraska, the Yellow River valley is like Colorado, and so on. And like the States, China suffers for its size: sometimes it is very hot, other times very cold. The region we were moving into was not as cold as, say, Chicago or New York were at that time of year, but was cold enough, the wintertime temperature of Washington.

I was eager for my first sight of the coast. I went to the bow, as far forward as I could before the sleek and polished deck degenerated into forbidden ropes and chains, and saw that the water ahead was stained a different colour. I could explain that, I realised, and, glad to be a guide again, I went to look for Roscoe. I thought he had killed his father, but I still wanted to impress him.

'It's the Yangtze does that,' I told him, pointing to the red-grey stain spreading across waters otherwise only grey. 'It washes down tons of soil every year; it moves the equivalent of an island of silt thirty yards wide and ten miles long.'

'You're a mine of peculiar information,' remarked Roscoe. 'All right: what can you tell me about the boats?'

A fair question, I guess, for the sea was full of boats, all following the course of the stain. The junks were archaic, like something from a comic opera; the ocean-going liners were smart and white and wore their colours on the funnels like knights' shields; the merchantmen and freighters travelled in shades of grey and black; the rusty tramp steamers were tatty and snug like old shoes. 'There's a lot of them,' I said.

And then the shore appeared, to the south, a yellow strip of land barely more solid than the waters. This was China then: my birthright; my homeland.

Or at least, I hoped it would prove that way.

Detail increased as the ship sailed in closer. We passed marshes, and dune-like ridges topped with half-hearted shrubs. Behind this was a swamp that reflected a patchy sky, and sometimes the waterbirds rose up there like mosquitoes. I stood at the rails with Roscoe and the ship pressed calmly on.

Shanghai is not on the Yangtze but on a tributary, the Whangpoo, and where the two rivers meet is Woosung, which was the first Chinese town I saw.

We passed a railroad, clearly visible on the flat estuary landscape, the locomotives elevated on levees, and saw a port. More interesting, more alien, were the houses clustered at the water's edge, their roofs angled and entwined as if a rush mat had been laid over scattered bricks.

The narrower Whangpoo concentrated the river traffic, and Shanghai emitted a short-range traffic of its own – ferries, river-taxis and water pedlars – making navigation slow and awkward. The water-salesmen called up to the ship, offering silk and bracelets.

The population on the banks increased even more than that of the river, and the two merged into one at the roadstead, where many people lived permanently in sampans. There were no longer significant gaps between either the buildings on the shore or the boats on the river; the only spaces were the narrow rights of way. I watched the activity on the dock. The cranes swung their loads; the coolies heaved their bales; the pedlars pedalled along the waterfront road. Stacked and packed on the side were bundles of silks and cotton, barrels of vegetable oil, knotted parcels of skins, animal fat in moulded blocks, and regular bricks of tea; resting on the parcels were the more delicate items, the jades, embroideries, porcelains and eggs of the interior, ready for loading on boats. Behind were the factories, whose tall chimneys were turning out tough, smoky streamers that dragged along in the slight breeze. It was a busy impressive place; it was less Oriental than Chinatown, San Francisco.

The Bund was a wide quay awash with people. I saw

cars and rickshaws and people competing in a teeming, turning reel. There were beggars displaying open sores, and rickshaw drivers fighting for fares. I saw well-dressed Chinese gangsters, as smooth as their watered hair, and their bosses' chauffeured limousines with the heavy, distorting, bullet-proofed glass. And I saw bodies floating downstream, pudgy in the water, the suicides and the unwanted daughters.

We put ashore. A car from Westhouse Oriental was waiting for us. So was a crowd of newsmen, in European suits and derby hats. They carried spiral-bound notepads and Swiss cameras and they recorded Roscoe's words and his moves. We crossed the Bund in a crossfire of questions. 'What do you think your chances of beating the Roosevelts are?' 'Will the death of your father affect you do you think?' 'What are your feelings about going into the Interior now the Kuomintang are so powerful?' 'Did you realise' – ho, ho, ho – 'that you were under suspicion?' 'Could you smile please? Please smile.'

We were news, and I had never been news before. I was not altogether sure I disliked it. I enjoyed the bustle of the newsmen, and their sense of purpose. Maybe it was then I found my vocation? It certainly took me a few years to realise it though.

Eventually we made it to the waiting vehicle. Roscoe shook hands with a burly man and we were introduced. 'Mr Greaves, Edmund Sin. Edmund, this is Red Greaves, President of Westhouse Oriental.' We climbed in the car. The chauffeur drove us away.

Leaving the newsmen lessened neither the noise nor the crowd. Travelling through Shanghai is like being continually mobbed. The evening was beginning and, driving slowly, the horn sounding constantly, we watched whole worlds unfold.

The Chinese shopkeepers hung banners outside their shops. The banners told the shopkeeper's name; the sort of shop was indicated by the colour of the flag. It took no skill to recognise most shops though. We passed fronts heaped high with blocks of tea, like builders' yards, and sharply scented restaurants, and once, unbelievably in that press of people, a blacksmith's. Were there really horses in Shanghai?

We moved on, and saw the silver-plated rickshaw of a night-club singer. The owner was being handed up to it, and her pearl-and-silk dress bubbled like freshly poured soda-water. We saw handsome policemen, Sikhs, bearded and brightly turbaned. There were dance halls now, and opium dens, open-fronted parlours where scrawny pale Chinamen puffed at pipes and ornate jars, and our senses were all alert despite the isolation of travelling by automobile. In the streetside cafés old men played mahjong, while pimps pushed their whores on the sidewalks, holding the painted women by the arms or the hair and thrusting them at the passers-by. Night dangled before us, temptingly, and I swear the city grew warmer. Lanterns were lit from the balconies outside the bars, luring beggars and fat pale moths. Shiny compradores, the indispensable Chinese lieutenants of the Western businessmen, haggled in the brocaded brothels. They looked like they were in on a racket; everyone in Shanghai looked like that. Pedlars peddled milk from slung buckets that were paired up on yokes like scales: ask for milk and they laughed and produced wads of dope from inside pockets. Old European matrons, emigrées from this war or that revolution, offered their daughters to the Cantonese business community and the businessmen established the girls in hotels. Reliable servants, the ubiquitous 'boys', off-loaded their masters' surplus goods and over-ordered to ensure the surplus. Even the girls who begged on the sidewalk, displaying decayed and stinking feet that had been disfigured by foot-binding, offered their misery like a commodity. There was nothing in Shanghai that could not be bought, or sold.

This did not feel like Home.

10
Shanghai

We were ten days in Shanghai. The first day after our arrival, December 15, Roscoe took me to a man we had been told about by the American Museum of Natural History, a missionary who had worked in Szechuan for several years until the Nationalists drove the Western missions out. I had not wanted to go because I feared I might be confronted with my ignorance. But Roscoe insisted, on grounds which were unanswerable though inaccurate: he wanted the missionary and me to compare and coordinate our knowledge.

The missionary lived in a bungalow in the International Settlement. It was a tree-lined, residential area, and we knew we had found the right place because a sign by the mailbox read 'Donated by the Charity of the Mission Society of West Kelp, 1917: Blessed is the Lord'. We got out of the Westhouse limousine and the driver clicked his heels. There were roses in the garden and lilies by the door.

Roscoe got to the door and it opened. The 'boy' who opened it wore a scarlet jacket with a white cross on the breast, and his hair was plaited. We went in. He showed Roscoe through to the parlour but made me stay in the lobby. 'You'd better wait,' said Roscoe. 'I'll send for you in a while.' I sat down on a chair and the boy made me stand again.

Roscoe was with the missionary perhaps an hour. The boy left: I heard him in the kitchen. I decided maybe the first chair I had chosen had been valuable, so sat in a different one. I guess I dozed. When I awoke the boy was scolding me shrilly in a ham, broken English he must have learnt in drama school. 'No sit! No sittee! You no sit! No sittee!'

I started to stand; he continued to scold. The missionary came through from the parlour, followed by Roscoe. 'What's going on here?'

'He sit! He sittee!'

'Did he!' The missionary was a powerful white-haired man with a good face and bad teeth. 'The impudence!'

'I tell him no sit! I tell!'

'Good boy. Not like this scoundrel. We should have him thrashed.'

I had made it to a sort of defensive vertical by now. 'I meant no disrespect,' I told him.

'No disrespect! Where'd you learn that? Bah!' He turned on Roscoe. 'This is your fault, Hamilton. You've got to keep them down. Look at Chan here. He's kept down. He doesn't even know what disrespect is.'

'He bad! I tell him no sittee! He bad!' confirmed Chan.

'Perhaps I should introduce you,' said Roscoe. He was trying not to smile. 'This is Edmund Sin, a graduate of Cornell . . . '

'Sin!'

'Edmund Sin.'

'Get out. Both of you.' The missionary spoke in low, forceful tones. I waited for him to say, 'I'll not have you bringing Sin into my house,' and was disappointed.

'Pleased to meet you,' I said as we left.

The chauffeur had the door of the limousine open; he was polishing the inside of the ashtrays. He stood straight for us and clicked his heels again, then rushed round to start the motor. I could feel Roscoe's laughter building up, and as soon as we were clear of the bungalow it burst.

'That was marvellous,' he said, through guffaws.

'I'm glad you enjoyed it.'

'Didn't you?'

'Sure. I just love being insulted.'

'It was his way. I shouldn't let it bother you.'

'I won't.'

I thought that was the end of the conversation. Roscoe settled back and composed himself; so did I. Then he started to laugh again. 'You should have heard the things he was saying about you. He told me he never trusted a Chinaman with shifty eyes. Apparently you've got about the shiftiest sort of eyes going.'

'Thanks. He never even saw me till he threw us out.'

'Chan told him.'

'Right.'

'He said the Chinese are the most despicable race on earth, so I told him you were an American. That made it worse, he said. That made you a turncoat.'

'You're making this up.'

'Would I do that?'

I did not know, so I did not reply.

'Edmund?'

'Yes?'

'Where's West Kelp?'

'God knows. But I can see why they paid to send him here.'

The second day I went to a tailor and had a suit made. It was ready for me by the evening, and a man on a bicycle brought it round. Pearl grey silk, it seemed marvellously elegant, with long European-style lapels and three fly buttons. I only needed a dark shirt and light tie to look like a Shanghai gangster.

I was young enough to want to go out in my flash suit, of course, and had heard about the Shanghai nightlife. I went round to Roscoe's room but he was staying in. There was an engineer fixing up a tickertape machine in his room: Roscoe had some messages due in from America. He asked me if I felt like gambling a couple of hundred on Wall Street, to take advantage of having the machine, but he could have meant a couple of hundred thousand so I ducked out.

On my way downtown I passed a stall that sold books. Many seemed to be about learning English if you were Chinese; how about one for learning Chinese if you were Chinese? I enquired: the bearded proprietor found the very thing, small enough to fit into my pocket. I took it with me to the club.

My suit was not the success I had hoped. Every Chinaman in the place was wearing pearl-grey silk: we looked like one of those teams of Oriental athletes at the opening of the Rome Olympics. Nonetheless, the singing was good and the food was superb, so I felt the evening left me in credit. I had a vague, Parisian longing for a woman, but neither the nerve nor the skill to acquire one, so before midnight I returned to my hotel room, riding back on a rickshaw, which was fun, and began to teach myself Chinese.

The book was called *Commercial Mandarin Thirty Two Lessons*. I was not sure I wanted to learn *commercial* Mandarin, strictly, but the book had an authoritative grey card cover and was written by Professor Chung, whoever he was, so I decided to make a start. I opened it at Chapter One, 'Speak', and read: 'Chinese word are always monosyllable. Kung is speaked like Gung.'

I shook my head, returned the book to my pocket, and wished I could have shown it to Roscoe. He always enjoyed the absurd. But I did not see quite how I could justify owning a book called *Commercial Mandarin Thirty Two Lessons* when part of my job was to work as a translator.

The third day was quiet. Roscoe was out all day, discussing his plans with the American officials in Shanghai, and after walking around the town a while, marvelling at the richness and the poverty, I returned to the hotel. I found myself playing poker with the filmcrew. They were a fairly indistinguishable crowd, I found, except for Frank Wetherby and his nose; Frank Wetherby must have found me fairly indistinguishable too, I guess, because he kept addressing random Chinese, regardless of age or sex, as 'Edmund'.

The fourth and fifth days were similar. Roscoe had found himself caught up in a social scene which entirely excluded me: I was more of an alien in China that I ever had been anywhere else: Chinamen were not popular in the International Settlement where the Westerners lived. On the sixth day, however, I was at last able to make myself useful. Westhouse Oriental had chartered a French-owned steamer to take us up the Yangtze. Commercial Mandarin I might not have mastered; the French language was no problem. I busied myself translating Roscoe's instructions to the crew, and found myself virtually supervising the fitting out, which was quite interesting: I had never really witnessed the *power* of money until I saw how Roscoe's reduced every problem. The owners said fitting the boat out would take four weeks; we achieved it in four days.

The seventh day was Christmas Eve. It was the day my wife was born, and while I guess her story should be a separate one I will tell it briefly here, because I am realising more and more as I write that this is not Roscoe's story, nor the pandas', but is mine, and I am sufficiently egotistical to like things this way.

My wife then: she was born on Christmas Eve 1927, and was seventeen years of age when, on August 6, 1945, the atom bomb was detonated above her and Hiroshima.

She was a typist. She worked in an attorney's office near the centre of town, but that day she had been given time off because her boss was sick and there was little work for her.

The war for Europe was over. I had flown back to the States. I was glad the Nazis had been defeated, sorry the British and the French and people like that had won. I was in Washington, DC, when the bomb was dropped. I guess maybe we saw the flash but that it took time for the shock-waves to reach us, for the first reaction was jubilation. American know-how had won through again: with a clean, modern, up-to-date weapon we had put an end to the filthy, old-fashioned war. We were so glad about the bomb we dropped another one, just to make sure.

The bomb exploded at 9.15 in the morning, Hiroshima time. The attorney's typist, queuing for provisions in a small suburban store, was lifted bodily some sixty feet in a heat-blast so intense it smeared the flesh from her exposed neck, arms and legs. She flew over the street and the army trucks that paraded outside, and landed by a miracle in an open water tank behind the houses opposite. She was terribly burnt, terribly shocked, terribly naked, terrified. But she was alive.

Later, the American people began to question the decision. Important people, like Oppenheimer who had worked so hard to make the bomb happen. Concern became public and widespread, and America looked for ways to make amends.

When the attorney's typist, who did not burn to death and did not drown, pulled herself out of the tank and climbed down the inspection ladder to the street, she found the street had gone. The buildings were mostly standing but had been derelict a long time now. The trucks were wrecked. She was confused and worried, as anyone would be. She told me that at that stage she felt no pain.

It was decided in Washington that aid should be given to the survivors of the bomb, the mangled, irradiated, scorched ones who had somehow made it out of the devastation.

The attorney's typist, the woman who would one day be my wife, wanted to go down-town. She never quite explained why: I think she believed she should be at work. The backs of her calves and lower arms had been

138

pretty much burnt away, and she did not get very far. She collapsed at the foot of the ladder.

The most publicised idea to help the Hiroshima victims was the one about the 'Maids of Hiroshima': a group of young women was taken to the States for the best in medical treatment and plastic surgery. I guess the idea was that treating them made us feel better. They were news for a while and then they were not news, but an editor I worked for suggested maybe it would make a good Christmas story if I could interview some of them and get them to say how grateful they were to the States for all it had done for them. I was more sceptical than he was, but I went along.

I interviewed several of the girls. They *were* grateful to the States. Then the nurse told me it was the birthday of one of them on Christmas Eve. She would be twenty-one. She thought I especially ought to interview that one. So I did, and wrote the story up for *Life*. Our wedding might even have made the cover if Ike had not accepted the Republican party nomination the same week.

I know why she married me: I was all she had got. And perhaps I even know why I married her, though that is harder to explain. Certainly, it had little to do with love, or even her; it was to do with America, manifest destiny, reparation and colonialisation. In my idiosyncratic, alienated way, I was trying to do my piece for my country. The love I felt for her came later, came too late.

Christmas Day was the eighth day of our sojourn in Shanghai. Roscoe was invited to a party. The film crew all seemed to be going to parties too, but no one invited me. I did not much mind. There had been too many parties.

Instead, I decided to go for a walk. I wore my gangster's silk suit. I walked miles, had dinner in a restaurant where they gave me Chinese food with American names – 'Chop pork stir fry; cooked rice; good cake' – and, by nightfall, was on the Bund. The Bund was uncharacteristically empty. It was good to walk there and see the buildings. It was good to get away from people for a while. I set off along the Bund's width, humming a carol for Christmas. 'Good King Wenceslas', I think.

I walked slowly, admiring the boats moored against the quay. It was a warmer night than it had been, and I had just taken off my hat to stretch the band when two men from the shadow of a nearby ship stepped out and sapped me.

I dropped to the floor before I knew what had happened. I was more aware of the pain in my knees than the sock on my head. I lay there dazed but conscious, my awareness more that of a man about to be sapped than of a man who has been. There were hands going through my pockets. I felt my wallet go, and my pens, and anything else I carried. Then they were pulling at my tie. It gave, but so did some of the stitching. It was only when they got my shoes off that I realised they wanted more than my wallet. I decided I ought to do something. I decided wrong.

The first kick caught me in the stomach. The second landed in my groin. They took my trousers and jacket with no trouble after that, and then they went.

Shanghai was an international port in those days. I did not even know what race my attackers were. But those boots felt Western. They felt agonising.

Time passed. I realised I did not have the faintest idea what I should do. I knew I ought to move. I knew I did not much feel like it. I do not recommend getting sapped, but at least it made me less conscious of my predicament. I wondered vaguely what the time was. I looked at my wristwatch and saw only wrist. They had taken that too, of course.

Voices approached along the waterfront. I was in shadow, for which I was perversely grateful. A man, beaten up, in his teeshirt and shorts, finds curious things to be grateful for. I could hear an American voice. Two figures came into my line of vision. The American was a sailor, in white. With him was a Chinese girl. They were arguing. His voice was a gruff Yankee rumble, hers a shrill and incongruous English Cockney. She kept repeating, 'I can hear you, I can hear you, I can hear you.' He kept saying, 'Then listen, will you? Just listen. Just you listen.' I wished she had listened. She might have heard me too. Instead, they passed into the night.

Several times other people came by. I waited for the next American. He was a long time coming, and when he came he was drunk, staggering theatrically and singing snatches of popular songs. All on one note. I let him pass.

I was getting cold, starting to shake, when I saw a man in a turban. I had been in Shanghai long enough to know that a turban meant a Sikh, and a Sikh meant a policeman. Come on Sin, I told myself: time for action. I stood up, shakily, and took a step forward from the shadows. 'Help,' I muttered; I did not feel like shouting. A lot of my confidence had gone with my clothes.

In good English he asked me, 'Who's there?'

'I've been robbed,' I said.

'Where are your clothes?'

'They were taken.'

'I see.' He had a rounded, pleasant pronunciation, and a way of dipping his voice round the vowels that might have been enjoyable to listen to, some other time.

'Could you help me?'

'You had better be staying where you are.'

'You will help?'

'Of course.'

He was gone maybe ten minutes. When he came back he carried a large blanket. 'Where are you living?'

I gave him the name of the hotel.

'It is a long way,' he told me. 'Wait here.'

'Again?' I asked, aghast, but he had gone. At least he had left the blanket.

The next time he returned he had a bicycle. 'You must

141

be riding on the back of the bicycle,' he told me. And so I did. I sat on the saddle, trying to keep the trailing corners of the blanket out of the wheels, and he stood while he pedalled. Away from the commercial districts the streets were as crowded as ever, and he rode well, pinging his bell ferociously at the dawdling pedestrians. Twice loose folds of the blanket wrapped themselves round the chain, derailing it, and each time the chain fell off so did we, but he was patient with me and never remonstrated.

Outside the hotel the limousines queued in dark lines. 'Can't we go round the back?' I asked.

'Why?' he wondered.

He rode up on to the sidewalk and stopped directly outside, clambering over the crossbar while I clutched the saddle and clutched the blanket and wished desperately I was someplace else. I could see civilisation through glass swing doors, and the Sikh policeman talking at the reception, and then a voice behind me spoke.

'Edmund,' said Roscoe. 'What the hell have you been doing?'

It had become hard to explain. I did not even try. 'Merry Christmas?' I asked him. He frowned.

They made me stay in bed the next day, which was my last full day spent in Shanghai. I was not badly damaged, but my head hurt when I shook it. 'Don't shake it then,' advised the English doctor.

I lay beneath white sheets. The room was high-walled and the ceiling carved into a mock-Baroque. A fly was making his way across the plasterwork like he had lost something, and he became the most important part of the Baroque design, incorporated in it and dominating it.

I closed my eyes reluctantly that night, knowing I would not sleep because of the hurt in my head and the excitement I felt about our journey the following day, and when I woke up it was morning and my head felt fine. A chambermaid brought me a cup of smoke-flavoured China tea and I got up and dressed. For the first time I put on my Expedition Outfit: khaki shirt with big patchpockets; khaki breeches ditto; short jacket, mustard colour and ditto; high boots of dark brown leather, not ditto but part of a dark brown leather set of straps and bags and pouches that had been explained to me in Macy's when I bought them and were now completely incomprehensible. Does the inch-wide strap go over the left shoulder or round my waist? God knows. And what am I meant to put in all these pouches anyway? I can't put cartons of cigarettes in them all.

We went to the boat in rickshaws, in a long procession of Americans that started with Roscoe and worked its way through to the most junior assistant and the most insignificant cameraman. I was annoyed by the way Frank Wetherby, his cigar-butt jammed in his face like a plug, took precedence over me, but could do nothing about it. I guess I was out of temper though.

The boat was moored at the Westhouse wharf on the far side of the Whangpoo; we crossed the river by ferry. On the far side we were greeted by an obsequious Chinaman who introduced himself as Westhouse Oriental's chief compradore. Although twice my age he was my height and build. More significantly, he was wearing my suit.

I did the classic silver-screen double take. 'You're wearing my suit,' I told him.

He replied in Chinese.

'Why are you wearing my suit?' I persisted.

He smiled defensively, uncertain of my status with the great Mr Hamilton. The great Mr Hamilton, however, was busy supervising the unloading of his guns and ammunition. 'Perhaps you go to the same tailor? Many suits like this in Shanghai.' Which I knew to be true. 'Maybe your suit like this?' I noticed he was slipping into pidgin, which I was learning was the domesticated China-man's way of playing possum.

I was undecided but unconvinced. 'Let me have a look at it,' I said.

'All suits the same,' he said.

This was absurd. 'I want a look.' He stared aggressively at me; I stared aggressively back. I had read more hardboiled novelettes than he had though; I knew the terminology. 'Hand it over, buddy.'

He shrugged elaborately, took off the jacket, and gave it to me.

I had not owned the suit long enough. I really could not tell if it was mine. And then I found *Commercial Mandarin Thirty Two Lessons* in the inside pocket. I presented it triumphantly, waving it in front of his face, and the compradore turned and ran. This was a surprise. Compradores do not often flee. They are very important people; they virtually run the commerce of Shanghai, controlling the Western companies while their white masters play polo or go to the races. When a compradore does flee, therefore, not many people know how to respond.

The tradition of American democracy has certain advantages over all other systems. Americans are not much worried by rank. One of the film crew, Chas Norbal, made an instant move to intercept the running compradore. More unexpectedly, and perhaps more com-mendably, one of the smart Westhouse chauffeurs joined in the chase. But the compradore was quick, and eluded them both. We set off in pursuit down a narrow dockfront street.

The east side of the river is not as prosperous as the west; it is mostly where the coolies live. We ran through poor streets that were unpaved and had to be negotiated by leaps from large stepping stones; between the stones was a foul mixture of fouler things that urine had turned to a constant slime.

We could see the shirtsleeved compradore ahead but

could not catch him. The chauffeur led, Chas Norbal was second, and I was third, until Chas fell into the filth between the stones to come up gasping and stinking and scabbed with dirty rice. I stepped over him and carried on the chase.

We were gaining. On my own I would have lost him, but the chauffeur was quicker than any of us, and more mobile. We passed through an open market, and the crowds slowed our quarry down, narrowing the distance, till we at last caught him. At the same time, Chas caught us. 'If I'm going back filthy I'm going back with the prisoner,' said Chas. I grinned at him breathlessly and realised I was smoking too much.

Red Greaves had arrived at the wharf by the time we returned, and was talking to Roscoe. He turned to us. 'Good. Han, now you're back, explain this nonsense please. I gather you're meant to have stolen a suit.' His voice was scornful: he knew there had been some mistake, and that his compradore would have a perfectly good explanation.

I butted in. 'It's my suit. He's still wearing the trousers.'

'I've known Han since I first came out East. Of course it isn't your suit.'

'How do you know?'

'I think we pay him well enough for him to be able to buy his own clothes.' Greaves looked at me. 'Why should he want to steal yours?'

'I didn't say he'd stolen it; I said he was wearing it.' But I was losing ground; Greaves's confidence in his compradore was absolute, as I suppose it had to be, given the nature of the relationship. Compradores have to be trustworthy, because they have to be trusted: confidence is vital in business. Then I remembered my evidence.

'All right!' I produced Exhibit A with a flourish. 'Then why was there a copy of this in the pocket?' I waved *Commercial Mandarin Thirty Two Lessons* between

Greaves's fat face and Han's thin one. 'Mine!' I told them.

'Han,' said Greaves with dignity. 'I think you should tell us about the suit.'

'I got it from a friend, said he knew where I could get cheap suit, good silk, brand new, no problems. No one says it is stolen. How should I know? I am a compradore. I earn plenty. If I had known it was stolen I would not have bought it.'

His English improved with his confidence. 'What about this?' I said, drawing his attention to the book. 'Didn't this make you suspicious?'

'I did not check the pockets. I would have thrown that rubbish away if I had found it, I think, if I was guilty of knowing the suit to be stolen.'

He had a point. I changed tack. 'I would still like my suit back.'

'I will have another made. I will take it to a tailor, Huang; he will make a copy. It will be ready for your return to Shanghai.'

And there we left it. I was cross. I was cross because I had thought to get my revenge on the thieves. I was cross because the compradore had not explained why he had run away, and yet had somehow explained himself out of trouble. I was cross because Han had apparently won our confrontation, making my concern for my suit seem petty and trivial. And I was cross because at no time had Roscoe taken my part, but had watched the whole affair with sardonic amusement.

Han took the jacket back off me, graciously bowing his head. He could not fool me though, I thought: I would have taken bets that he was up to his neck in illicit deals, and had run because he feared he was drowning.

The *Chanson*, our river-steamer, was freshly painted but otherwise dated. She had a tall old-fashioned funnel and a flat deck on which the superstructure sat like stacked boxes. She was not a big boat – a big boat would have been unable to navigate the higher reaches of the Yangtze – but as we sailed beneath the bows of the moored ocean craft our horn still scattered the sampans like they were floating leaves.

The weather was poor. A thin dampness clung to the land, too insubstantial to be mist, too wet to be ignored. Visibility was reduced to maybe six hundred yards. I stood at the rails next to Roscoe. 'You nearly made a fool of yourself there,' he told me.

'You didn't help much.'

'I guess not,' he agreed.

'That Han's a hood,' I said, chasing my grievance. 'Otherwise why did he run off?'

'Of course he's a hood. That's how business is in Shanghai, I guess. That's how business is everywhere else, for sure.' He put a hand on my shoulder. 'You're a natural comic, you know that? Just about everything you do makes me laugh.'

I was not sure I liked being his jester, his fool. The First Officer of the steamer walked by. 'Where are we stopping tonight?' I asked him, in French. I wanted to reassure myself, and prove to Roscoe, that I had a serious function on this expedition.

'No need to speak French. I'm from Stateside myself,' said the First Officer, laughing. 'I guess we haven't met: I'm Bill Young; I was up in Nanking when you were fitting the tub out. If ever you need any translating done with the crew you can come to me. If ever you need anything.' He winked. He had a good wink, slow and salacious.

'Thank you very much,' I replied coldly, but then the sun came out. What the hell, I thought, and I turned and looked at China.

11
The Yangtze

I stood at the bows and stared, and found wonder in all I saw. Two hundred million people live in the Yangtze valley, more than live in all the United States. Two hundred million people: two hundred million lives; lives happy and hopeless and humdrum and done, just like everyone else's.

The villages crowded the riverbanks, and between the villages were flat rice fields. The fields were divided by canals. I could see water where, in more familiar landscapes, there would be roads, fences, hedgerows and paths. Water dominated here. The river gave the landscape meaning; the canal network spread the river's influence.

This bureaucracy of canals pried behind the houses, revealing the villages' innards and their flabby butts. From each house a flight of steps dangled down to the water, and at the foot of each flight, like bait, there was a kneeling woman. The women were washing, mostly. They scrubbed at the garments, humping them up and down in the water or beating the filth out with a stick. Soap in China was expensive, and watching the women thump at their clothes, I saw why the Chinese use buttons of cloth.

The women who did not wash clothes washed vegetables. They held them under the water or filled wicker baskets with rice. Strings of curious ducks kept paddling up to the rice baskets to peck there, and boys tied loops to the ends of bamboo poles to lure the birds away from the food. The lines of cheerful ducks, quacking and following the noose, were like a crowd on its way to a hanging.

And then the boat had moved past, until the next village, and I was left with thoughts that were like old photographs, unnecessary and sometimes inexplicable, but made special by the shutter's click.

Two hundred miles up-river we left the Pacific tides. The river was still two miles wide here, and slow-flowing, ponderous. We passed Nanking, the new capital of China, where Chiang Kai-Shek held court; we did not put in there, for the Nationalists did not welcome foreigners, but sailed past while Roscoe cleaned his guns.

There were hills to the north of us now, and gradually the landscape changed. Six hundred miles above Shanghai we reached Hankow, which is a big port at the place where the Han joins the Yangtze. From the river Hankow looks a little like Shanghai, for it has a European Bund, but behind the Bund it is purely Oriental. I had my first Chinese girl in Chinese Hankow. Her name was Judy.

I met her at a club used by riverboat officers. The First Officer of the *Chanson* took me there while Roscoe stayed aboard and looked at maps. 'Ed,' said the First Officer. 'You look like the type can appreciate a woman. Maybe you'd like Judy?' He introduced me to her in a pidgin English that reduced what he had to say to an advert from a personal column. 'Edmund here nice Chinese boy from Chicago wants company, wants good time, savvy?'

'One dollar him get plenty good time,' she replied. I have never understood what made pidgin happen: it's more complicated than standard English.

'Sure thing. One Yankee dollar?'

He was teasing and she knew it. 'No American dollar. Silver dollar.' The silver dollars came from Mexico: for some reason Mexican dollars were the most acceptable unit of currency in China at that time.

'What you reckon, Ed?' asked the First Officer. 'Is she worth a silver dollar?'

I did not know how to measure. I still don't. 'Sure,' I said.

'Right. That's fixed. I'll leave you two to get acquainted.'

We danced a little. The dancing was difficult; the band played awful jazz and Judy had no interest in the steps. She was a plain pleasant girl with a professional smile that was fifty-fifty enticement and boredom. We hardly exchanged a word. When the music stopped we went upstairs.

There were booths on the next floor. Each had a mattress and a chair. She lay on the mattess while I folded my clothes on the chair and then, as we used to have to put it in the litigation reports for the newspapers, intimacy ensued. If you want the details read someone else, someone younger. Suffice it to say that I shot my seed in her Chinese womb and because of this, sexually, symbolically, sentimentally, stupidly, this became a significant moment in my life. All China had opened her legs for me, for the price of a silver dollar, and the foul Hankow jazz as I returned down the stairs made me dance.

The First Officer was waiting. 'You were a long time,' he said. 'I've had three women while you've been gone.' I suppose he was lying; I hoped he was. 'We ought to beat it back to the boat now. I guess you can let me have a couple of dollars for finding the girl for you?'

'Oh, yes.'

'Great. Ten'll do. We'll see what we can do for you at Ichang, up the river. If you're lucky I'll get you Lucy. Classy dame.'

'I'm not sure.'

'Very clean. Always wears fancy French underwear. Great legs.'

I am a sucker for fancy French underwear. 'I'm still not sure,' I said.

'Look. Let me have thirty dollars now and I reckon I can guarantee we get you Lucy. That sound okay?'

150

In the end he took thirty-five. Maybe I am just a sucker, period.

We steamed on. We passed paddy fields. A boy led a docile herd of water buffalo to the river: they floundered in the shallows and wallowed cheerfully where it was deeper; like all China that I had seen, their happiest element was water.

We passed a honey-boat. The honey-boats carried the night-soil, the excrement, from the towns to the fields. Night-soil was an important resource in the Yangtze valley, where there were too many people and too few fertiles areas; I do not know how much night-soil was reaching the fields that day though, because as the honeyboat rocked in our wake fat brown-green smears slopped over the side, to float corruptly or to sink in a froth of sluggish bubbles. I thought of the women washing vegetables, and then tried to forget the thought.

Another snapshot: naked children swimming with grave untutored strokes down the canals. I remember a confusion of longings: I wished for a moment to be with them, playing; I wished too for my own childhood, and for the first time I had first swum a length of the echoing pool of my father's Chicago club. I guess somewhere on each journey we always travel into the past like that: sometimes I think my life has been spent collecting more nostalgia than experience.

And one final photograph, before we reached Ichang and the gorges: the cormorant boats sailing at dusk.

We watched the boatmen push them out, like gondoliers, while the cormorants perched on the side of the boat, mere passengers. And then the fishing grounds were reached, so the birds flapped their heavy wings. As birds they were rookies; as fish they were superb. They hit the water like torpedoes, emerging perhaps twenty seconds later with self-satisfied expressions and their throats full of fish.

'Why don't they just fly off?' I asked the Second Officer, who was half-Chinese, half-Belgian.

'They've rings around their necks,' he replied, 'to stop them swallowing the fish.' He was about my age. We spoke in French, and he seemed glad to be able to answer my questions.

This was as well; I had lots to ask. 'But how does that stop them escaping?'

'They know they can't eat with the rings on,' he replied. 'And the only people they know who will take the rings off are their masters.'

The simple ingenuity impressed me. There seemed a metaphor in this that would serve for all oppression: we serve and love those who merely take the rings from round our necks and let us eat.

It was soon nightfall. The cormorants were punted back to the shore, and we moored away from the banks, in case of bandits or Nationalist troops. We had papers from the government which were meant to allow us passage, but many of the Nationalists were very zealous, and not all of them could read.

'I wonder where the Roosevelts are?' I said to Roscoe.

'There's no need to worry,' he said. 'We'll beat them.'

I was glad of that.

We entered steep close hills before we reached Ichang. The town was walled. Szechuan junks lined the water-front. Ichang is a porcelain city in a China cup of hills, and on the facing bank is a cliff that buttresses mountains.

The Second Officer pointed a hill out to me. It was pointed, regular, slab-sided and apparently artificial. He assured me it was natural, and that its dimensions were exactly those of the Great Pyramid.

'Weird,' I remarked.

'Yes.' He pointed in the other direction, showing me an elaborate monastery that faced the Pyramid Hill. 'The natives think so too. That's why the monastery is there, so

152

that the monks can pray against the Hill-Demon.'

'What you telling Ed all that for?' asked the First Officer, also in French. 'That's not what interests him.' He gave me his wink.

Roscoe remained in his room, but I got off the craft. The First Officer took a tender through the high-sterned junks, and we climbed stone steps to the quay. As we did so, a coolie on a bicycle came riding by, ringing a handbell with one arm and steering with the other. His vaudeville English carried across the quay: 'Tellyglam for Misty Am-Ill-Tuan! Tellyglam for Misty Am-Ill-Tuan!' It was with difficulty, and with a laugh, that I realised the wire was for Roscoe. I paid no particular attention; Roscoe was receiving mail all the time, wherever we went. Rich men lead more than one life, for their interests are spread far and wide.

Lucy had the good legs and the French underwear promised, but there was no sense of achievement this time, no epiphany. I cannot remember her well; I do not want to remember her well. I left instead with a feeling of loss, for it seemed I had not penetrated China after all.

'No more women,' I told the First Officer, and he smiled and told me about a place he knew in Chungking.

There was a creek that ran into the Yangtze to the east of Ichang, and that was where the poorest people lived. There were families dressed in rags there, standing in doorways, watching the impatient world. Many of the shacks were on crude platforms above the creek, but the very worst were beneath these, mere wigwams of coarse matting on the mud banks at the river's edge. We passed quickly by, and the rich even-tempered smell of opium drifted through an air that was otherwise disease and rot. I could tell the opium smokers: their eyes were full of silence.

Ichang was, I think, a beautiful city, yet I found no beauty there.

We returned to the ship, where the First Officer found himself in trouble. 'Who gave you permission to go ashore?' demanded the Captain.

'We always go ashore at Ichang,' protested the First Officer. 'We've got to go ashore to refuel.'

'M. Hamilton has received a telegram. If you had been alone, and not taken M. Sin, we should have left without you.'

'I'm sorry,' he said. 'How should I have known though?'

'You know who M. Hamilton is, I suppose?'

I worried about that telegram as I went back to my room. I felt I ought to apologise to Roscoe for holding the boat up, but I did not feel I could face him. I thought I knew what the telegram must contain; I thought it would be the news that the alibi provided by Michael Hall and Paula Jaycee had been exposed as a lie. I thought it would prove Roscoe's guilt.

Suddenly the landscape reared, and we entered the Gorges. The river was confined between great cliffs which spilt and split the water into rapids and made it roar like blood in frightened human ears. All around us echoed spray and noise, as though violence itself had volume.

And this was winter: this was the low water, the quiet time of the year. Later, when the snows of the Himalayas had thawed, the river would swell to many times its winter size. In the Gorges it could only rise; there was noplace else to go. Sometimes the level went up by hundreds of feet in a few hours, making navigation impossible. Then the flood would pass and the level would drop: once a steamship had moored overnight in such a flood; when morning came it found itself perched a hundred and twenty feet above the next day's waters, and I guess it is there still.

I have been nowhere on earth so potent. I was in a land of high cliffs held apart by a slice of tiny, inaccessible sky.

All my life I have been an outsider, an alien, but all men are outsiders in the Gorges.

I returned to the saloon and got a drink. It occurred to me that I did not know what day it was, which, at that time of year, meant I had also lost track of the year. I guessed 1928 must have begun, but that seemed kind of irrelevant. All human measurement seemed that way: it was probably January 4, I decided, but to give the day a date in the company of the Yangtze Gorges seemed audacious.

Our Western dates are a fairly arbitrary scheme anyhow. According to the best authorities, Christ could not have been born in Year One: we either accept Matthew's testimony that the Flight into Egypt occurred in the final year of the reign of Herod the Great, which was 4 BC, or we assume Luke's statement to be correct, which places Christ's birth in the year of the census, which was AD 6 or 7.

The Year One was devised by a certain Dionysius Exiguus, a Greek-speaking monk who lived in Rome. Basically, he got his calculations wrong. Nonetheless, in my opinion Dionysius Exiguus remains a major, and undervalued, figure in European history: for Dionysius Exiguus devised the system whereby the West dominates the world.

Most peoples, tribes or nations do not measure time sequentially. Their calendars tend instead to be cyclic. In China, for instance, there are years of Goats, Crabs, Cats and so on; in Ancient Rome it tended to be 'The Third Year of the Pro-Consulship of Marcus Scullus'; in many other countries a memorable event was the basis for the dating, such as 'The Year of the Big Tide' or 'The Month of the Hunger'.

The Western calendar is different. One Year of the Frog is much like any other; in the West, not only is 1963 different from 1928, it is measurably different. I can count out the years of difference, measure my own decay and

155

the world's dubious 'progress', calculate that we have had thirty-five years' worth of change. The sense that things *should* change is an implicit part of the Western calendar and the Western way of life, and is responsible for the activity with which the West learnt to dominate the world. We make faster cars, smoother tobacco, bigger bombs, because our calendar demands these improvements.

'We make', I have written, and 'our calendar': despite my complexion and my blood, I share the Western concept of time rather than the Oriental one. In the East time is a pool of still water in which we float until we drown; in the West it is a flood that kills us unless we keep striving.

I stand up, go to the washroom, fetch a glass of water. My sense of time is confused now; I cannot tell if these were the thoughts of 1928, or thoughts that happened a moment ago. The water is cold and hard, and tastes of pipes and tubes. I trundle it round my mouth, letting it lift my single, cunningly-disguised denture. Time in the West is always the enemy; if I am to finish this tale by my sixtieth birthday, my self-imposed deadline, then time is running out.

Roscoe joined me on deck. 'What happened to you?' he asked.

'In Ichang?'

'Yes. We nearly left without you. You heard about the telegram?'

I admitted I had. 'Was it very bad?' I asked, trying to think about what I was saying, trying to avoid saying what I was thinking.

'It depends. I wish I knew more about their plans. It looks like it's become a straight race.'

'I don't understand,' I said.

'The Roosevelts have reached Chengtu.'

'Oh. That's what the telegram was about.'

We were silent some time. The river's noise made

talking difficult anyway. I looked up at Roscoe and saw a smile beneath the surface of his face that was as hidden and as clear as nakedness between sheets. 'What are you thinking about?' he asked.

I decided I would have to say what I thought. 'I thought it was about your father. About his death.' I paused. 'Michael Hall and Paula Jaycee couldn't have been together on that island when he fell in, could they.'

'Of course not. But even Katherine isn't tough enough to brazen that one out.'

If I looked puzzled I guess he put it down to the difficulty of hearing above the sound of the river.

We were three days in the Gorges, learning to get familiar with the wonderful and the strange; and when we finally emerged in Szechuan it was like emerging into daylight after a tunnel.

Of all the provinces of China Szechuan is the most crowded. Yet it was not a sense of crowds but of openness I felt after those Gorges. And despite the vast numbers, people seemed subordinate to agriculture everywhere I looked.

We passed a tall pagoda, the first I had seen in China. Its segmented walls were a house of cards, and in the background the regular Szechuan hills rose and fell like a green counterpane over a sleeping child. The sun was out. Birds flocked. The river, in a tame mood between the spring floods and the angry Gorges, flowed by. But I was not happy, not really. I was in the heart of China now, and too busy looking for Roscoe to think of looking for me.

Roscoe had been spending a long time studying his maps. He had some the missionary had sold him, others supplied by the Museum of Natural History, and a particularly useful set the US Army had provided. 'What are the roads like in Szechuan?' he asked me.

'I don't know,' I replied. 'I've never been this far up the Yangtze before.' Which seemed to me better than telling a direct lie.

'Really? I guess it doesn't matter though; I'm sure you'll still be able to help. The problem is we're making lousy progress. If the Roosevelts were in Chengtu when we were in Ichang they'll be half-way up the mountains by now. At this rate they'll have killed a panda before we get within two hundred miles. But what if we go overland from here, rather than going on to Suifu as planned? The Yangtze curves a long way south from here, and we want to head due west. But would it be even slower to go overland? That's the nub of it.'

'I don't know,' I admitted.

'Go on,' invited Roscoe. 'Give me a decision.'

I wanted to stay on the river, I felt: I was safer there; there was less chance of my ignorance being exposed. But Roscoe wanted to be the first white man to kill a panda – I don't know why; I'm not a white man – and going overland did look quicker. 'It'll depend on what kind of transport we can get,' I decided. 'But it looks quicker cross-country.'

'Good. I'm glad you agree. I thought you would: you're a gambler; we first met in Monaco, remember. And you wouldn't have come on to this expedition if you weren't prepared to take a risk.'

He was in a good mood, the result, perhaps, of nearing the end of his quest. He laughed at me. I laughed, a little uncertainly, right back.

'Mind you, I guess going overland could risk you making a fool of yourself,' he said. I stopped laughing. It was not hard. I felt my belly heavy inside me as he continued. 'Still, I was sure to discover you didn't know China some time.'

He was still grinning.

'How long have you known?'

'Since England.'

158

'Good grief! But why didn't you say anything? Why did you still bring me along?'

'I kind of like having you around, I guess. And I admired the way you hunted me down in England.'

A suspicion occurred to me. It was a time for frankness. 'It wasn't to get me out of the States?'

'Out of the States? I've heard of the White Slave Trade, but you're the wrong sex. Hell, you're not even white!'

'I'm talking about your father's death.'

'I'm not following this too well, Edmund.'

'I'm the one who knows Michael Hall and Paula Jaycee were lying.'

'Well, of course they were. But Katherine was hardly going to own up to being with him on the island. Hall and Paula will be paid off, I guess. They'll be all right.'

It was my turn not to understand. 'Katherine? Your wife? But she wasn't there either. She was with me. They all were.'

'When?'

'When you killed your father.'

'When I did what!' He looked at me in horror.

'I understand,' I said. 'He was talking too much; he was drunk. I guess it was an accident. I won't say a word.'

He turned away from me. I thought it was guilt; it was sorrow. 'Edmund,' he said without looking at me. 'Edmund. I thought we were friends.'

'You can trust me.'

He turned round. 'Trust you! Edmund, for Christ's sake, how can I trust *you*.'

'God, I'm sorry about the deception. But we are friends,' I said. I was so certain I was being noble and sensible. 'You can tell me.'

'How long have you been thinking this? No, don't bother to answer. Look, Edmund. Let's get this straight. I did not kill my father. I didn't even see him. You met him on the lakeside, he fell in the water, and my wife and Michael Hall just happened to have been nearby at the

time. They didn't know it was him. They didn't really
know it was anybody. They didn't know because they
were balling. Have you got that?'

I imagine I just looked blank.

'Have you got that?'

I nodded for him. He shook his head. 'You don't even
deserve an explanation,' he said. 'Not after the way
you've been doubting me. But I'll give you one all the
same. Forget my dad: he's just some poor drunk who
walked into a lake, and if that doesn't sound too pleasant
then I'm sorry, but that's how I've always felt about him.
The important thing at that party for me was that
Katherine was there. I hadn't seen her for some time:
she'd been living in LA and hoping to divorce me, but I
didn't want that.' He lit himself a cigarette. 'It's all to do
with money. If I desert her, or commit adultery, or
something like that, she'll be able to take me to the
cleaners. But if it's her that's at fault, I'll not need to give
her a cent. That's why she threw Paula Jaycee at me the
night of that party.'

'But why did she say Paula had been with Hall on the
island? Why did she need to say anything? If you'd been
arrested I guess she could have got her divorce some way.'

'She's not that kind of woman. She wouldn't do that to
me.'

'God,' I said. 'I was so sure you had killed him.'

'Forget it. I guess it must've looked kind of odd from
where you were standing at that.'

There were still things I did not understand. 'Why did
Paula Jaycee go along with all this?'

'Money.'

'And Michael Hall?'

'The same. Hall might even love Katherine; Katherine
might even love him, though I don't really believe that.
But they both of them love money more. I can understand
that. Katherine's used to money: her entire life is shaped
by money. Losing that would be like dying for her.'

'Why don't you just divorce her?' I asked.

'I don't know. I need evidence still, I guess, but that shouldn't be hard to come by. Perhaps I will.' He did not look happy at the thought; I could not understand, but then I did not learn to love my own wife until she was almost dead.

'Roscoe. I'm sorry.'

'That I screwed up my marriage?'

'That I thought you'd killed your father.'

'There's nothing to be sorry about. I often enough wanted to kill him.' I decided he was joking because he laughed.

'But I should've known you couldn't have killed him. Look: I'll get off at the next town, make my own way back home. I'll get off now if you'd prefer.'

'What are you going to do? Swim for the shore? Don't be dumb, Edmund: we've got pandas to hunt.'

And I did not learn to love my wife until she was almost dead.

12

Szechuan

We had reached the centre of China, and I was glad to be there. I was glad to be through with the play-acting too. I felt I had nowhere further to go now; but for Roscoe, the expedition was only just beginning.

We disembarked at a town called Wanhsien. Our arrival attracted a lot of attention, and the crowd that formed pressed around the boat. It was impossible to gauge their mood: they could have been inquisitive, aggressive, or downright felonious. We retreated to the steamer.

'Could you talk to them?' the Second Officer asked me.

I shook my head and felt ashamed.

'I will talk to them then,' he said.

He climbed on to the poop and rang a handbell. When he had their attention he spoke to them in the local tongue, South-West Mandarin; I took some consolation from the thought that probably none of them spoke Commercial Mandarin anyhow. The Second Officer's name was Jean Chan, and I guess he promised the crowd money, because they began to look cooperative. And then, ironically, I became a translator after all, translating Roscoe's instructions into French before Jean could pass them on to the crowd.

'Is there any chance of a truck?' Roscoe asked. I translated his question to Jean, who was organising the unloading.

Jean looked thoughtful, and then excited. He ran on to the quay to do some more bosswork.

'Did he say what he had in mind?' asked Roscoe, but he hadn't.

We soon found out. Within half an hour there was a line of ancient, dilapidated boxes on the quay. Each was about a yard square at the base and five feet tall; many bore the remains of fancy paintwork. 'Family-size coffins,' said one of the film crew.

'Sedan chairs,' said Jean Chan.

'Where on earth did you get them?' I asked.

'They belonged to the Mandarins. Then there was the revolution. Now they belong to the people.' The people had been keeping chickens in them, judging from the stench.

'The revolution was fifteen years ago,' I said.

'Sixteen.'

'Are these chairs still sound?'

'Enough will be. We only need seventeen.'

It was my turn. 'Sixteen,' I said. There were fourteen in the film crew, plus Roscoe and me.

'Seventeen,' Jean insisted. 'Including me.'

I gave Roscoe the gist of this conversation. 'Good,' he said. 'Ask him who's going to carry the chairs.'

I passed this on. Jean opened his arms wide in an expression he had probably learnt from his Belgian mother. 'Tout le monde,' he said. 'There is no shortage of people in Szechuan.'

I looked around us. He was right. The streets were full of people; the terraced hillsides above the streets were full of people; the canals that wound between the terraced hillsides above the streets were full of people too. There was a face in every window, a figure in every doorway. Brimless velvet caps bobbed over the bridges; broad-brimmed, pointed coolie hats made barnacles along the waterfront.

'What did he say?' asked Roscoe.

'Tout le monde,' I repeated. 'All the world.'

We left town the following morning. We were a walking carnival, a parody of a parade. There must have been

163

nearly two hundred of us: Jean had organised teams of five to carry the chairs, one of whom was resting at any time, and many other coolies were employed as porters. Overnight, the selected chairs had been cleaned and patched up. They used bamboo for the poles to carry them, and cushions were found for the seats. Valuables, such as Roscoe's guns and the movie cameras, were carried in the chairs with their owners, while the rest of the luggage was strapped to the coolies' backs.

I tried to work out how much it all cost. The Captain of the *Chanson* had made no objection to letting his Second Officer go that a few hundred dollars could not solve. The coolies were earning five Mexican dollars apiece, which, according to the intricate rates of exchange in operation along the Yangtze, meant something like twenty or thirty dollars a head; the hire of the sedan chairs was presumably more. In addition, there was the cost of food and accommodation along the way. In other words we crossed Szechuan for, at my estimation, around $5000, which was less than our Shanghai hotel charges.

It was good value for money, and left everyone satisfied. Five Mexican dollars was more than most coolies would earn in a year. Jean enjoyed himself enormously finding the right people and the right route, while Roscoe and Frank Wetherby talked about the publicity value of this for Westhouse.

It is time to talk about guns. I had not really seen Roscoe's shotguns until he took them from their cases to carry them in his sedan chair. I had expected Westhouse 'Modern' repeaters, the guns that had won the West; instead, these were quite different weapons, with oddly cumbersome butts and complicated sighting mechanisms. I asked him about this once when we broke our journey.

'The "Modern" is a Two-Two,' said Roscoe, stretching.

'I'm afraid I don't know what that means.'

'A jack-rabbit rifle then. Two-Twos are light and versatile, but not what you need against big game.'

Roscoe had used a 'Modern' himself, to shoot the birds from the ship, but I did not mention that then. Seagulls are not big game, and anyway, it was a subject I wished to avoid. It was the dark side of the sun. 'When I was a kid the cowboys in the picture books all used "Moderns".'

'That's publicity for you.'

'You mean they didn't!' My American heritage was affronted. The 'Modern', like the Winchester and the Colt ·45, is part of our history, after all.

'I wouldn't go that far. Somebody must have bought them, I guess, or we couldn't afford to be here. But you wouldn't use one against buffalo, for instance.' He stood and stretched again. The sedan chairs were rather cramped. 'I'll show you something. Tell Jean to wait a while longer.'

He went over to where the coolies rested, opened a long wooden crate stencilled 'Westhouse Corp', and pulled out a sleek, familiar Westhouse 'Modern'. In a different box he found several rounds of ammunition. 'Go find a rock about the size of a hen's egg and put it on the roof of the chair. And get Jean to make sure everyone stays clear, in case there's a ricochet.'

I found a rock and placed it where he wanted. 'Stand well back!' he called. With a swift, relaxed movement he raised the rifle, let out his breath, and fired. I had forgotten how quick he was with a gun, and how good.

'Now go look for the rock,' he said.

It was about thirty feet from where I had placed it, but easily identified by the clean scar that marked one face. 'Put it back where it came from,' he instructed.

This time he used one of his game guns. There was the same quick lift of the muzzle, the same exhalation, and an even louder report. When I went to look, there was no rock left. Just dust, still settling in the mid-morning sun. 'If a lion's going for you,' Roscoe told me, 'you have to stop it with one shot. A Two-Two can penetrate a lion's heart but it won't always stop him if he's made up his mind to pounce. A Two-Two means you might need a second bullet, and often there just isn't time. He'll be on you, and you'll be dead, and after a while he'll be dead too, in an agony he doesn't deserve.

'So we use a game gun, and stop him with one shot.'

We made very good time, covering around fifty miles each day. The coolies seemed invariably cheerful: if they were earning more for these few weeks than they would normally get for a year, I could see why. I wondered what we were doing to the local economy.

As we travelled, the horizon altered. Szechuan is sometimes called the Red Basin because of the colour of its rock. We were continuing our journey West, towards the mountains that mark the far border of the province, and every day the range, which had begun as a line of white, like a mist, grew first into a cloud-bank and then into something more permanent.

'It was the mountains attracted me most to this idea,' said Roscoe. 'I did some mountain shooting in India a few years back. I guess these are the same mountains, really.' He was quiet a while, looking at them. Then he smiled. 'Let's get Frank Wetherby to take a few shots. It's time he earnt what I'm paying him.'

And so we became filmstars again. We stood in front of the backdrop of distant mountains, or in front of the procession of sedan chairs, while the film crew set up their tripods and viewed the world through their squares of blue glass.

'Roll,' called Frank Wetherby, and things rolled.

It is a shame the film was never printed.

Most nights we stayed at inns. There were no inns big enough for all our party, of course, but the coolies seemed happy enough to rest beside walls or under bridges. I began to understand something of the white men's attitudes to the Chinese when I thought of our coolies: they

166

were so uncomplaining, so docile, so unambitious, so numerous. I began to understand that attitude; I began to share it. I hope I know better today.

I do not know if all men are equal. I do not know all men. But all those I have known had led me to believe in equality. Not equality of attainment, nor of ability. What we share most is our frailty.

There are two ways of coping with the knowledge of our frailty. One is by contempt. 'People are weak; people are contemptible. The weaker they are the more contemptible they become.' This is a narrow attitude. It ignores how weak *I* am. The second attitude is compassion. 'People are weak, and so am I. But if we join together we become that little bit stronger.' Our weakness becomes our strength; death becomes the spur to improving life. This is the only philosophy I can believe in, the only one that makes sense.

But I should return to Szechuan: I was talking about the inns.

For the second part of our journey towards Chengtu and the mountains we followed the Talu, the ancient imperial road that linked Szechuan and Peking. Although the road surfaces were not particularly good, we could still recognise the road as an amazing feat of engineering. In particular, it was very well served by inns.

Generally, the inns were all of the same design. The sleeping quarters were half-timbered, and the windows round, so the effect was of a Hollywood fantasy on Shakespearean England. Attached to this was a cross between a lean-to and a verandah, within which the customers sat. The customers were travellers, always. There were no neighbourhood bars or cafés, as in the States or in France. Perhaps this was because there was not much drinking in China, nor much to drink. There was no wine, because there were no grapes: the choice was between a clear spirit made of barley or millet, or a rice beer.

Despite the absence of neighbourhood drinkers there was a sense of community, encouraged by the feeling that each inn was the same as the last. Certain things seemed to apply wherever we stopped. For instance, Szechuan is inhabited by almost as many mosquitoes as it is people. The landscape is full of canals and irrigation ditches; mosquitoes love canals. They also love inns, so in each one there seemed to be a customer dedicated to the task of filling the area beneath the verandah with smoke. The mosquitoes hated the smoke. I agreed with the mosquitoes.

Likewise, the superstitions were much the same from inn to inn. In each there was a pigsty on the ground floor. Sleeping above the pigsty is said to bring good luck. It was strange how often I was the one who got the good luck, and the sleepless nights that went with it. It was not just the stench, it was the noise. Fertility is a characteristic of the whole province, and the pigs were no exception. They were at it all night, every night.

In time we reached Chengtu. Outcrops of the mountains fingered their way towards the huge city, making it hilly and handsome despite its size. Jean, who had relatives there, found us a hotel, but the governor had heard of our arrival and invited us to stay with him. After weeks in ex-chicken coops, all we cared was whether there was a bath.

Roscoe's first priority was to discover where the Roosevelt brothers were. He found they had set off for the mountains about a week earlier, and that a telegram message from Weiku, in the valley of the Min Ho to the north-west, suggested they had already found traces of the panda in the vicinity. Roscoe sent off a couple of wires himself to tell the world where we were.

'Would you do me a favour some time, make up for your suspicions about me?' he asked.

'Of course I would.'

'Well, you're a scholar: do you think you could write up this trip some time?'

I am trying.

He continued, 'I wouldn't like to think I could pass straight through this world without being noticed.'

'There's not much danger of that.'

'Who was William H. Harrison?'

'I've never heard of him.'

'He was the ninth President of the United States,' said Roscoe. 'So much for fame.'

That evening we went to the governor's party. I had promised myself no more parties, but I guessed this one would be different. I had never been entertained by an Oriental dignitary before.

I was right about the party. It was different. Our host didn't wear a tuxedo, he wore a white tie and tails.

The food was also Western, which was a relief. Szechuanese food is the most highly spiced in China, and I had not really developed a taste for it. At the table I was next to the governor's wife, who spoke excellent French: her father had been a diplomat. We had a clear, flavourless consommé, and then the conversation turned, inevitably, to Roscoe's expedition.

'How many men are you taking?' she asked.

'There are seventeen of us. We are all here. And we shall see if we can find a guide nearer the mountains.'

'I have met your seventeen,' she said with a charming smile, and I realised with surprise that this was the first woman of my own race I had ever had a conversation with, apart from my mother. 'But they are all film-makers like Mr Wetherby or companions and helpers like you and Mr Chan. Where are the hunters?'

'Mr Hamilton is a hunter.'

'Mr Hamilton is a very famous hunter. But surely he does not expect to track down and kill the panda on his own. The Roosevelt party was smaller, but they had trackers and hunters with them.'

'I really don't know,' I said. 'Did you meet the Roosevelts when they were in Chengtu?'

'They stayed, yes.' She gave me an even warmer smile. 'They did not speak French as well as you.'

We talked a while about Paris, where she had lived as a girl. I told her only pleasant things that might match her memories. Then the conversation was interrupted by the arrival of the next course, which was delicately cooked carp, served in what seemed to be a béchamel sauce. 'Sometimes my chef, who is from Chungking, does not altogether understand *haute cuisine*,' admitted our hostess. 'The Roosevelts did no better, I am afraid.'

'I've heard a lot about them, but never met them. What are they like?'

'They are like brothers,' she said. 'There was a Tibetan called Cutting, who is quite famous in the mountains, and a big-game hunter called Jack Young with them. Jack Young has often been to Chengtu; you probably know him yourself, as he is an American.'

I smiled at that. 'Roscoe will,' I said.

Roscoe was talking with the governor. They spoke English. The governor was telling him of the Lolo tribesmen who lived in the mountains. 'Beware them,' he said. 'I gather you have had no trouble with bandits yet.'

'No.'

'Then you have been lucky. After the Warlords surrendered earlier this year, which is when people like me, Kuomintang men, modern men, were installed, a good number of soldiers deserted. Whether they feared they would be punished for the crimes of their masters, which is not the Kuomintang way, or whether they just decided they could do better on their own, I do not know. Many of them have become outlaws. Yet no Chinese outlaw is as dangerous as the Lolos. Where you are going, into the Tahsueh Shan, they are terrible. I would not venture there myself. These Lolos are cannibals.'

'Thank you very much for telling me,' said Roscoe.

We left the following morning, leaving the sedan chairs and many of the coolies in Chengtu and travelling north along the Min Ho, the river that feeds the Chengtu plain. Szechuan itsclf does not suffer from frost: its growing season is ten months of the year. But we were soon in the foothills of the Tahsueh Shan, the Great Snowy Mountains, where white trails of snow marked the paths between the winter trees like snails' trails.

Behind us was the Chengtu plain, spread as richly as honey. We climbed with the sun that morning, and the dawn sent scarlet lines along the canals. They seemed to be heading West as the sun escaped over the mountains; they seemed to point out our route.

All around us was birdsong, like a wind orchestra tuning up, playing snatches of the tune, never quite grasping the need to play together. Either that, or it was modern music, an accompaniment devised by Berg or Schoenberg. Many of the trees were evergreen where the birds inhabited the branches like leaves, marking and mocking our progress. When we stopped we were tired but felt good.

'I've asked Jean if he can arrange your journey back to the States, Edmund,' said Roscoe.

'What do you mean? Aren't I going back with you?'

'No. I think I'm staying on.'

I looked at him. 'Then I'll stay too.'

'No you won't.' He gave me his most boyish smile. 'Can you spare a cigarette for me?'

I gave him one. He cupped it under his hand to light it, like a soldier. 'Why can't I stay?' I asked. 'I'm not doing anything else.'

'I know. I'm sorry. But if I have a companion at all where I'm going, it'll have to be someone who knows the mountains. Someone who can hunt.'

'I see. An Uncas, a Chingachgook.'

'Exactly! And I'm sorry, Edmund, but let's face it,

171

that life wouldn't suit you.'

'It might,' I said, stubbornly. 'I've not tried it.'

He was no longer really thinking about me. 'Do you know how often a man as rich as me gets to be alone?' he asked.

I thought the question was rhetorical but he seemed to want an answer. 'Not often,' I hazarded.

'That's right. That's why I want these mountains.'

'This is where you're going to stay then?'

'Higher up, I guess. I want to shoot the last big game first, and then I'll find a settlement or something, to begin with. I haven't really made many plans; I won't know what I'm going to do till I get there.'

'It all sounds pretty half-baked to me.'

'It probably is.' He grinned. 'I'll probably change my mind about it all. You know something? The real freedom of having as much money as me is that it allows you to change your mind.'

Jean was urging the coolies to their feet. We were soon under way again.

After several days' travel we reached the point where we would have to cross the Min Ho. The river was strong and wide; the bridge was neither. It was the sort of crazy construction Tarzan habitually eschews in favour of a liana in the movies, and looking at it I could see why.

'We're going to cross that?' I asked. Frank Wetherby was busy asking the same.

Roscoe could not see what we were getting at. 'There is another bridge a few miles north, but I think we've gone north far enough. I don't see the point of going any further.'

Frank Wetherby and I did, if the bridges were better, but Roscoe had already started to cross. The coolies seemed happy enough following. I followed the coolies.

The only consolation I could find in the situation was that at last I had found something I could agree with

Frank Wetherby about. This did not seem much compensation for being suspended two hundred feet in the air on a bridge that was floored mostly with holes and suspended from what looked like long but badly rolled cigars. It was bad enough that the whole thing shook with every step that I took; it shook with every step that everybody took, until it bounced like a telegraphist's forefinger.

At last I got to the other side. 'Right,' said Frank Wetherby. 'Mr Hamilton, Edmund, just go back out to the middle of the bridge will you, and walk this way with the cameras rolling.'

It is possible I swore.

Ahead of us, the Great Snowy Mountains made a pathway to the clouds. There did not seem to be a pathway down.

13

The Tahsueh Shan

I heard it on the radio. Kennedy is dead. I was finishing my tale; I knew exactly what would happen next. Now Kennedy is dead, and my story is changed.

It has become so unimportant it does not seem worth completing, so significant I hardly dare finish it at all.

We entered the Tahsueh Shan, the Great Snowy Mountains. They folded and creased above us and from a distance their whiteness made them insubstantial, reminding me of thrown-away paper or the firs in my parents' garden after snow. These innocent images were not adequate however: the peaks thrust through the undergrowth like sharks' fins in a bathing pool. Then our path began to climb, and the mountains became substantial as well as dangerous.

We climbed through trees that were heavy with water. The trees made the day darker; the branches licked us as we passed and our clothes darkened too. We passed through blossom gardens, wild roses, acacias, rhododendrons, maples, pines. Ivies and vines wrapped the trees. Running water, running loudly, running risks, found routes down the slopes. And everywhere there was bamboo, its sectioned stem like garden furniture, its tufted head a barbarian spear.

The first village was in a valley. It was a Chinese village; the Lolos lived higher in the mountains. Roscoe had various letters of introduction from politicians and museums and academic bodies. For the first time in our journey he needed to use them: it seemed we had moved beyond the range of Westhouse Guns. He handed them to the village headman, but the headman could not read. We were told to wait for the return of the headman's son.

Time passed in a lazy, unhurried way. America – cocktails, tickertape and coupés – was far behind us now, but so was China. We were beyond the telegraph and the smell of decay. Courteous people showed us where we might sleep: a large round hut with a hole in the walls to let in the people and a hole in the roof to let out the smoke; there was a shelf round the walls to sleep on, and no other furniture.

It was soon dark in the hut. The sun had gone: the light through the hole in the roof became diffused and half-hearted. Roscoe left us without saying anything; I sat around for a while unable to think of anything to do, then followed him out.

I looked around but could not see him. The villagers were fetching in their herds, and I watched the skinny sheep, more goat than sheep, being funnelled into pens. No one seemed very interested in us, despite our movie cameras and our guns; we were here and we were guests, and they would doubtless try to make money from us, but we were a long way from being a sensation. No one watched me, suspiciously or curiously, as I climbed above the village.

It was twilight now. I sat down and blew on my hands, for it was cold between the mountains. Sitting on a rock, looking down on the village, blowing into my hands in the twilight, I was reminded of the drawings of Greek pastoral scenes in my childtime book of Classical mythology. I shaped my hands differently, making a tight cup with the thumbs parallel, and blew into the space between the thumbs. It made a gentle, melancholic sound, the note of an owl or a night breeze rising.

'Hi!' said Roscoe.

'You made me start! I didn't know you were around.'

'Don't get up,' he told me.

He came over to where I sat. I whistled into my hands again, softly, and we looked at the mountains around us.

'It's beautiful,' he said, solemnly. 'Now you know why I brought you along?'

'So I could see this?'

He shook his head. 'That's crediting me with greater charity than I possess. No, I brought you along for my sake, not yours. You're a dreamer, Edmund, a romantic like me. I knew you would be the kind of guy who'd climb up rocks and whistle like the wind, and I wanted someone with me who'd understand that, who'd understand me.'

I stood up. I wished I did understand him. It was getting colder. I looked around the valley again, and then turned to look at him. He was standing in profile to me, watching the light fade away. His mouth was firm and content; his eyes were alert. He felt me looking at him and turned to face me.

'Hawkeye?' I asked him.

'You're still not quite Chingachgook,' he replied, looking at me, and suddenly we were laughing.

It was a moment of mad recognition, two sentimentalists sharing a sentiment, but it was a potent moment too. I guess had we lived in a different, more honest era, we might have embraced. Instead we continued to look at one another for a while, and then smiled and returned to the village.

The headman's son had returned by then. He was a short, dark young man who carried a rifle. He read each of the letters aloud and in turn, and the father encouraged his son proudly. It was quite dark before he had finished, and the stars were trivial between the mountains. According to Jean, the boy read even the names of the paper manufacturers printed on each sheet.

The earth moves rhythmically round the sun. It is the primary rhythm of all the rhythms that dominate our lives. The moon moves equally regularly around the earth. We count these patterns, subdividing into years, months, weeks, days, hours, minutes and seconds, and then name this system Time. But Time is not a matter of patterns and rhythms; it is not to be found in the rotation of moons or the fingers on a clock. Time is what happens to the human, and the human alone: Time is getting older, getting weaker. Time is what kills us in the end; it is Death's henchman.

Yet, though I believe Time has no objective reality, I continue to make spurious patterns with dates. Humankind's genius lies in the making of patterns in a random world; our tragedy is that we believe in the patterns we create. At the beginning of April 1928 I was in the Tahsueh Shan. Thirty-five years later, in April, my wife died of the cancer she contracted when the government of the United States of America exploded an atomic device above her home town. That government was chosen by the people, for the people. It was chosen by me, for me. Twenty-five million, six hundred thousand, five hundred and four people elected the government that killed my wife: did I kill her, or only a twenty-six millionth part of her?

Did her cancer start in my twenty-six millionth part?

More patterns. In 1928 Good Friday fell on April 6. William Faulkner's novel *The Sound and the Fury* is set that same Easter: while Quentin ran away and Jason tried to chase her, and Benjy burst into tears because Luster drove him the wrong way round the square, I was hunting pandas. Another tale of sound and fury, I guess, told by another idiot, court jester, court fool.

Or, finally, take today. Warren Harding died under mysterious circumstances. He died of food-poisoning though no one who shared his meals was ill at all. He died conveniently too, at a time when his reputation was good and his excesses unknown. I began this story on the fortieth anniversary of that death; I shall complete it on the day another President dies. I say I shall complete it, for although I planned to work tomorrow as well, I know now that today is somehow the end. On Sunday I shall be sixty (and Voltaire will be two hundred and sixty-nine); meanwhile today is Friday, another Good Friday, another day of execution.

We left the village, continuing west, and climbing the route the villagers used to herd their flocks from the mountains. Although we stayed below the snowline, as do the pandas, the snow sometimes came down to meet us anyway. The gullies were often snowfields, palmed like a pitcher's glove, and we crossed them in a monochrome line.

Roscoe called our new camp 'Hamilton Creek'. Familiar domesticated plants, azaleas and late crocuses, grew wild between the trees, and the stream that cut through the clearing was toothpaste sharp and clean, polishing the fangs and molar rocks. This was the hinterland, the place between the trees and the snow.

It was the most beautiful place on earth.

We were four days at Hamilton Creek, without finding any trace of the panda, and then we moved on, taking all our equipment higher into the mountains. We went through long bleak valleys that were calf deep in snow, and entered frozen forests that were wrapped in crystal, where the spring was still coiled and waiting; sometimes, suddenly, we would find a sheltered space, a few trees that were free of the ice and snow, and there the ground was shot with flowers of blue and yellow and white.

'I'd like to try up there,' said Roscoe, pointing to a goat-track that led up the mountainside.

'It'll be a struggle for the cameramen up that path,' I warned.

'We can do without the cameras. I've been filmed enough, I reckon. Standing, running, lying down; shooting, eating, lighting a cigarette. There must be more feet of film on me than Charlie Chaplin! I've been shot so many times I should be weighed down with lead.'

'It was your idea to bring the cameras.'

'A lot of things have been my idea,' he said. 'Now let's climb the mountain.'

Jean led the men along the valley; we climbed out of the shadow. The bamboos were bent with ice here, packaged up in brittle silver shells like Christmas. Then we were through them and had reached a plateau.

The cameras should have come with us: it was a world seen through a blue glass square, a cinema world, a camera world. The klieg-light sun spangled the snow and an eddying wind made theatrical flurries. I stood at the edge of the plateau watching the line of cameramen and porters we had left, and a snowball hit me on the ear.

'Got you!' cried Roscoe, grinning and ducking.

I turned quickly and scooped up a handful of snow.

'Where are you?'

'Here!' he called, and another snowball hit me.

'Right!' I ran after him across the plateau, finally thumping the ball into his back at short range.

It was his turn to come at me then. His pale lashes were flecked with melted snow, and there was a large piece of ice in his hands. He approached me ominously; I laughed and taunted and tried to get the hell out, but his grin was wider than mine and he dropped the ice on my head. I felt it crack in my hair and scatter down my neck. I yelped: and my yelp echoed round the mountains like the sound of a massacre.

Roscoe tried it. 'Cooooeeeee!'

'*Cooooeeeee!*'

'Hellllllooooo!'

'*Hellllllooooo!*'

'Is there anyone there?'

'*Air? Air?*'

'Is there anyone there?'

We made a snowman of two great balls of snow. Cartridges from Roscoe's belt made teeth and eyes. It was a formidable, ugly snowman, and when we had finished we knocked it down.

'We'd better get back to the others.'

'Sure.'

We returned down the goat track and found their trail. 'That was good,' announced Roscoe.

I agreed.

'I reckon it's this that made me a hunter. Freedom, and solitude. I need that solitude.'

But it was not the solitude I loved. It was the companionship.

We caught up with them in a quiet valley. It was well-wooded, one of those sheltered parts that avoided the frost, and the river that cut it had been dammed by a landslip. Jean supervised the fires and the tents. Frank Wetherby was filming again. We drank spiced broth from enamel mugs, and ate a casserole of rice and local lamb. I slept well that night, and slept long, and woke feeling great, for I knew he would not leave me to make my own way home.

We called the new camp 'River Dam'. The following day Roscoe took out a smaller party, with only one camera and half a dozen porters. We went West a while, into the shadow of huge mountain. It was cold there, and the snow was deep. 'We need more information about the pandas' habits,' said Roscoe. 'I don't know if they'd come this far out of the woods, but we've seen no sign of them near the trees.'

'I'd stay in the trees if I was a panda.'

'They might like the mountains,' said Roscoe. 'I do.'

We crossed a bleak corrie. 'I'm coming back here,' Roscoe added. 'When we've finished. There's room to breathe.'

A bullet smashed a rock by his feet.

'What . . . ?' I asked, but Roscoe had already moved.

'Get down!' he cried, taking cover behind a convenient

outcrop. I followed him as quickly as I could. Behind me, I heard our small party yelling and splitting up, and then the sound of another gunshot.

'The first bullet must've come from about there,' Roscoe told me. I was busy catching my breath. 'Let's see where the next one comes from.'

He stepped out of the rocks. There was another report, echoing round the corrie.

'I thought so,' he said, stepping back.

'Thought what?'

'That there'd be more than one of them.'

'Who are they?'

'How should I know? Communists, bandits, Lolos? Al Capone? The Roosevelt brothers trying to keep one step ahead? Let's just call them Hurons.'

I thought he was irritated by my question, but he was smiling.

I looked across the corrie. It was a good place for an ambush, a giant's toe-hold in the lower slopes of the great mountain, where we were overlooked from three sinister sides. In the centre of the corrie, comically upright, the movie camera was abandoned on its tripod.

Time passed. 'Just walk around out there a while, will you?' said Roscoe. I stepped forward but he caught my arm. 'I was joking,' he said.

'Oh.'

He stood himself. Another bullet sounded as he stepped out and as rapidly back.

'Be careful,' I said, inadequately.

'I'm all right. You can tell a lot by listening to guns. It sounds like they're using adulterated Two-Two ammunition, which means they're out to scare, not to kill. At this range, using a second-rate cartridge, they couldn't expect to hit anything.'

I had never been under fire before. I thought I was coping well: I did not seem to be frightened or panicked. The truth was I did not believe it was happening. There seemed nothing personal about these gunshots: they were sound effects, sound-track. We counted an hour on our watches and nothing changed.

'All right,' said Roscoe. 'Let's try again.'

He used his gun to lever himself to his feet and stepped out of the rocks. At once came a double report. The second shot was fatally close. I heard Roscoe's body thump into the snow, and then silence.

Numb time passes slowly. A bandit had crept in close, I realised. He had crept in close and waited. I could not accept that Roscoe might be hurt; I could not forget that he might be dead.

I looked cautiously round the rock. I could see his foot sprawled in the snow. 'Roscoe?' There was no answer.

I do not know how long I remained with my back to the boulder. Long enough for the words going through my mind to become a meaningless refrain. *Roscoe is dead*, I thought, *Roscoe is dead*; and the words, and the world, meant nothing.

At last I realised I must move him. Action fathers hope: perhaps he isn't dead; perhaps *I* can save him. Specious, baseless thoughts to keep myself going, maybe, but better than despair: before I could change my mind, revoke my hope, return to despair, I jumped from behind the rock. A bullet rang. I ignored it, concentrating only on Roscoe. There was no time to pick him up; I dragged his body by the ankles.

His weight resisted me but my fear made me strong. I pulled him into the cover of the rocks. A bullet chased me in.

'What are you doing?' asked Roscoe politely.

Nothing happened in my head. My mind was disconnected at source. 'I thought you were dead.'

'I wasn't.'

There was not much for me to say.

'I told you those rifles weren't accurate. I was just

staying out there, ready to return fire, when some guy grabbed my legs!'

'What about the bandit who crept in close?'

'What bandit crept in close?'

'I heard him fire. The moment you stepped out. I heard him fire and I heard you fall.'

Roscoe opened and closed the butt of his rifle rapidly. '*I* fired that shot,' he said patiently.

I am drawn away from the Buster Keaton routines of my youth. The BBC World Service delivers the news. The piecemeal story is being arranged by experts: soon they will have invented exactly what has happened.

'You can't say Dallas isn't friendly towards you today,' said the Governor's wife, but before JFK could reply he was hit by two bullets.

Roscoe and I waited another hour, then he walked out again. Nothing happened, so he waved me and I followed. Did Kennedy feel so exposed? Did he find spies in every window, assassins behind the news-stands? Or was he unconcerned and blithe and rapidly dead? The movie camera looked like a survivor of the Battle of the Little Big Horn; the corrie was fifty miles wide and a thousand deep, and Roscoe, at the other side, was stretching like a cat.

Our companions began to appear from their hiding places. We were two missing. It was not hard to find them. Their footprints led to a sombre black rock at the edge of the corrie mouth. They were naked, and their throats were cut: by each neck a red stain was melting the clean white snow. Their deaths made us small and foolish beneath the hills. 'I'm sorry,' said Roscoe, very quietly.

Death is like that. It reduces things. My wife's death turned her into a carton packed with faulty parts. Even the cancer that killed her was finished. We wrapped this package into another box and dropped it in the soil, and there my imagination falters, unable to confront her decomposition, her decay.

But the reduction was not confined to her. I entered this empty room and it remained empty, uninhabited, a comfortable coffin. My only plan was to people it with my past, and to finish writing before my birthday. For I thought I could start again at sixty, ha-ha, and be done with my past altogether. Now my tale is nearly over and my companions are leaving me again. Time has condemned me to solitary confinement; time is a subtle torturer. It tortured us in the long period of grief even before my wife died, when we watched the cancer grow. It tortured us through our love and our desperate hope. For it hung like the drops of water above a prisoner of the Chinese, and fell and drove us mad. Now I still have the love, though I have lost the hope, and the torture has been changed. Now I am quite alone, and time stretches like the rack.

Jean had news when we returned to the camp, and I did my accustomed translating. 'A Lolo hunting party came to see us. There are Communists in the hills; the Lolos thought we were government troops.'

'Were these Lolos unfriendly?' asked Roscoe. This was an excuse to stop thinking about the dead.

'No. They wanted help from our troops. When I explained that we had no troops and told them what we were doing they were surprised. They say the black and white bear is not worth the trouble. It is not to be eaten, and its fur is coarse.'

'What about the Communists?'

'The Lolos say this is a group new to the hills.'

'It's getting crowded,' I added. 'Perhaps you'd better keep away from here after all.'

'Maybe. Or I might join up with these Lolos. Or with the Communists.'

'Sure.'

The mountains kept becoming skyscrapers in my dreams that night, and tiny green-skinned figures defended the half-built Chrysler Tower against battalions of Communists who waved Red Flags and raped their own mothers for sport. I was especially clear about the latter because my dream featured newspaper headlines to prove it. When I woke the Lolo hunting party had returned. Their skin was not green but they were kind of stocky.

They reported they had found panda droppings: the stools had been traced several miles. I was enthusiastic, but Roscoe advised caution. The death of the porters the previous day had hurt him, though he did not speak about it. The expedition had lost its innocence.

'If you'd hunted as often as I have,' he told me, 'you'd know there are a lot of people who'll tell you what you want to hear.'

Nevertheless, we set out. The droppings were distinctive and copious: I am no expert on animal stools, but even I could recognise the effects of the pandas' curious bamboo diet. We followed the trail as far as the forest, where we had a hasty international meeting. Roscoe and the Lolos soon tired of translations of translations though, and because action really does speak louder than words, they set off together into the trees.

There was a long pause, a silence, and then, not far away, Roscoe's gun fired once. He never needed to fire more than once.

I ran into the forest, following the sound of the shot. Many of the porters came too, cheering and laughing through the trees. I guess they had been promised a bonus if we were successful.

The black and white corpse lay on its belly with its eyes open. It looked bemused by all the fuss going on around it. There was a bullet wound above its heart, and this had already attracted the hardy flies that live in the mountains. The only white marking I could see was a crescent on its upper chest.

185

'Well done!' cried Jean, using one of his few English phrases. 'Bravo!'

'Don't get too excited,' said Roscoe. 'It isn't a panda.'

'How do you mean?' I asked, while Jean, who had not understood Roscoe's reply, continued with his noisy congratulations.

'It's a black bear,' said Roscoe.

'A black bear? So there wasn't a panda then?'

'The droppings were genuine enough, I reckon. A black bear wouldn't leave marks like that. But I guess even if there was a panda round here we'll have scared him off by now. If my bullet didn't chase him away, the noise your gang made sure will have.'

We went back to camp. 'Friday 13,' said Roscoe philosophically. 'We should've known we wouldn't be lucky today.' Meanwhile, thirty miles to the south of us, the Roosevelt brothers proved him wrong by firing simultaneously and thereby sharing the distinction of being the first white men to shoot a panda.

They had been in the neighbourhood longer than we had and had travelled deeper into the mountains. But I believe it was the former that made the real difference, for like us they had made contact with the Lolos, and, as was to become increasingly obvious when the reports of the two expeditions were published in a special edition of *The Journal of the American Museum of Natural History*, the Lolos were of vital importance. It had been a Lolo huntsman who had drawn the Roosevelt's attention to an elderly male panda asleep in the bole of a tree. The panda was disturbed by the fuss and stumbled, half-awake, towards a line of bamboo. Whereupon they shot him, and wired the world of their success. We, who were within a few miles, were naturally the last to hear.

At length we found our panda's trail again, almost cold now but the only thing we had to follow. It led us north, towards the town of Somo which is deep in the Szechuanese Tahsueh Shan.

There was no sense of hunting an animal. 'We're just getting an idea of its movements,' Roscoe said. 'It must be three hours ahead of us at least, though these droppings are so dry anyway that it's hard to tell.' We walked companionably though silently for a mile or more. 'What did you think of my father?' asked Roscoe.

'I don't know,' was all I could think of to reply. What did he want me to say?

'Well, how did he compare to your father?'

'How did he what?'

'How did they compare? Your father and mine?'

'I can't answer that. It doesn't make sense.'

'Why not?'

'I knew one of them really well, as well as I've ever known anyone, I guess. I met the other twice.'

'But if you had known my father better?'

'Why are you asking all this?'

'I guess I'm curious. I want to know.'

We were still walking, ducking to avoid the frozen boughs or dropping quickly into the thawed world below the snowline. 'I just wonder how you felt when you heard he was dead.'

'*My* father, you mean?' I had to stop. 'I felt I'd killed him.'

'Come on,' he said. 'Keep moving.'

We walked a few hundred yards further. 'When I heard Dad was dead, I was scared,' said Roscoe.

'That's only natural. Whenever someone close to us dies it reminds us we're all going the same way, I guess. And we wonder how we'll live without them.'

'It wasn't that scared me. No, it was that I realised every time I'd fired a gun, I'd had my father's face in the sights.'

'Jesus!'

'It was worse than that. What really scared me was the

thought I might not want to shoot any more. With him dead, what would be the motivation?'

I had nothing to say.

'That's why I had to shoot those birds from the ship: I had to find out if I could still do it.'

'And could you?'

'Ask the seagulls.'

I would never be a huntsman, I realised, and I was glad.

'Hunting has been my life a long time. It started as the one thing I could do to please my grandfather; ended up the one thing that pleased me. I didn't really want . . . shhhh!'

We had entered a glade. 'What's the . . . ?'

'Shhhhhhhhhh!'

A panda, sitting on its fat butt with a piece of bamboo in its hand, watched us from the far side of the glade. It looked like a man dressed in fur. I heard clicks behind me, and the mechanical whirr as one of the cameras started filming.

Black and white film is beautiful. I have loved the echoing emptiness of images on the silver screen, and the loneliness of the shadow. Black and white film enhances almost everything, I guess, except for black and white bears. For the bear was truly black and white, and relaxed and decadent and quite at its ease. It took another bite off the bamboo stem; I expected to see it spit it out, like a man who chews tobacco would. Its belly was white, its legs and shoulders black. Its head was white too, save the eyes, ears and nose. Did the sons of Teddy Roosevelt really shoot such a Teddy Bear? Surely it reminded them of *their* father?

Roscoe raised the gun to his shoulder.

It was the shape of the head, maybe, and something in that confident posture; the panda reminded me of my own father. It watched carefully as Roscoe took aim. I heard him let out his breath to relax himself, as marksmen do before firing. Suddenly I wanted to scream. Dead fathers, dead presidents, filled my mind. I thought of Roscoe, killing his dad with every shot he had ever fired, of the Roosevelts slamming bullets into a big fat Teddy Bear, of the words I threw at my dying Americanised father.

Roscoe squeezed the trigger.

He fired.

He missed.

The panda, disturbed, vanished into the trees. Roscoe shouldered his gun and picked up his bag. 'I guess that's that.'

He walked across the glade, heading West. The camera followed him over the snow. He passed through a line of frosted trees and out the other side, climbing into the snowfields. I watched him all the time. He never looked back, though I had so much hoped he would wave. The camera tracked him until he went from sight, and then he was gone and the film had stopped.

I took off my mittens and wept.